truth

chasing yesterday

book one . . . **awakening**
book two . . . **betrayal**
book three . . . **truth**

chasing yesterday

book three
truth

robin wasserman

SCHOLASTIC INC.

New York Toronto London Auckland Sydney
Mexico City New Delhi Hong Kong Buenos Aires

For my mother

No part of this publication may be reproduced, stored in a retrieval system, or transmitted in any form or by any means, electronic, mechanical, photocopying, recording, or otherwise, without written permission of the publisher. For information regarding permission, write to Scholastic Inc., Attention: Permissions Department, 557 Broadway, New York, NY 10012.

ISBN-13: 978-0-439-93342-1
ISBN-10: 0-439-93342-0

Copyright © 2007 by Robin Wasserman

All rights reserved. Published by Scholastic Inc.
SCHOLASTIC, APPLE, and associated logos are trademarks and/or registered trademarks of Scholastic Inc.

Book design by Tim Hall

12 11 10 9 8 7 6 5 4   8 9 10 11 12/0

Printed in the U.S.A.
First printing, September 2007

damage

Her heartbeat stopped.

The green line on the monitor went flat. The dull beeps blended into a long, whining tone. The tubes dripped, the machines wheezed, but the girl — the body — lay still. Her eyes were closed, her skin pale, her lips dry, her lungs empty. One last breath had rattled through her, nearly silent, gasped out just as the monitors announced the end.

There were no alarms.

Two men stood by, one at her head, one at her chest. Each had a small gray device, the size of a calculator. It was all the weapon they needed — or had been, when the girl was alive. Now there was no need for weapons at all.

Seconds ticked by, and the men watched.

White straps pinned her swollen body to the metal

table. The sensors taped to her chest and head registered the vital details:

No respiration.

No pulse.

No neurological activity.

No signs of life.

The man by her head checked the clock. The girl had been dead for ninety seconds. He smiled. The clock ticked; the heart monitor continued its whine. Thirty more seconds passed. And the man by her head, the man in charge, nodded.

The other man pulled two paddles from a silver cart. He pressed them flat against her chest and flicked a switch. A bolt of electricity tore through the girl.

The body shuddered.

The high, thin tone droned on; the green line remained flat.

"Again," the man in charge said. The girl had been dead for one hundred and forty seconds.

And again, paddles met flesh, power surged, the body shook.

And again, nothing.

"Again!" the man in charge shouted. "Turn up the power."

"I don't think she —"

"Do it!"

The other man followed his orders and turned a dial all the way to the right. He clenched the paddles, breathed deep, and, hands trembling, lay the paddles against her chest.

The body shook and shuddered. Her back arched up, then slammed back against the metal with a dull clang.

Then the whine broke off into a chain of beeps, slow but steady.

And the flat green line turned into a mountain range of peaks and valleys.

And her chest rose as her lungs filled, then fell again as she breathed her first breath.

And the man in charge smiled and strode to the door of the small, windowless room.

"Wait until her vitals stabilize," he ordered, pausing in the doorway. "Then begin again."

Four days passed.

Four days since the girl had delivered herself to him.

Four days of waiting — impatient, impotent, interminable waiting.

Waiting and watching — and wondering if the project could be saved. If the girl could be repaired.

Ansel Sykes had supervised the treatment himself. Not even his most trusted confidants knew about the procedure he had authorized.

The procedure would not restore her damaged memory, nor would it restore the control he'd lost. Not right away. But if it worked, it would be a beginning. It would reset her. Like reformatting a hard drive, it would break down the resistance that had built up over the past two weeks, the weeks she'd been on the run.

He still didn't know what had gone wrong. He had sent her — his best subject, his prized possession, his special pet — into the field alone for a final demonstration of her skills. The test had gone awry, and when she'd resurfaced, nothing was the same. Her memory was gone, her abilities forgotten, his control erased. The reimplantation process had gotten off to a promising start, but it had been too slow. She had escaped.

And now that she was back, there was little time left.

No time for slow, safe procedures.

He had only a week to recreate what it had taken a lifetime to produce. Which meant pumping the poisons into her body all at once, rather than a little at a time, day after day, year after year. Which meant pushing her brain to the breaking point — and her body far past it. It meant taking a risk that the next time, or the next, she would not come back.

"Report," Dr. Sykes snapped as the man trembled before him.

Sykes sat at his desk, tapping his fingers lightly against the computer keyboard, struggling not to betray his impatience. The subordinate stood across the room, hands clenched tightly around a black clipboard. He kept his head down, refusing to meet Sykes's gaze.

They all preferred not to look at him.

"Vitals are strong, sir," the man said. "We've administered the final treatment."

"How long this time?"

"Excuse me, sir?"

Dr. Sykes pursed his lips. He couldn't stand incompetence. "How long was she gone this time?"

"Well, we had a little trouble. . . ."

"How long?"

The man checked his clipboard. "Three hundred thirty-seven seconds, sir," he said quietly.

Too long.

"But as I say, her vitals are strong now," the man added quickly. He deposited a report on Sykes's desk, then quickly backed away again. "She's received the full dosage of Lyseptican, just as you ordered, and her system seems to be tolerating it better than any of us expected."

"It's exactly what *I* expected," Dr. Sykes reminded him.

"Oh. Yes. Of course. I only meant —"

"We've done all we can do at this point," Sykes said. "The rest will need to be administered gradually. You've moved her to a recovery room and begun to wean her off the sedation, as ordered?"

"Yes, sir."

"How long do you expect it to be before she wakes up?"

The man paused. "Under normal circumstances? We would expect signs of consciousness within a few hours, and full awareness shortly after that. Anything longer would be cause for concern. But, sir, I warned you before. This treatment, there's no precedent — I can't be responsible for —"

"I'm well aware of the risks involved," Sykes snapped. "And you said yourself that the indications are all positive." He drummed his fingers against the latest report. "Heartbeat — strong. Breathing — unassisted. Brain waves — within acceptable parameters. At least, acceptable for *her* brain."

"The machines can tell us only so much, sir. Until she wakes up, we can't know how well her brain has coped with the oxygen deprivation and the repeated shocks to the system. You should be prepared. Even if she regains consciousness, there's a chance, a good chance, that she won't be . . . well, there's no guarantee of a full recovery. I just want to remind you that we won't know anything until she wakes up."

Sykes closed his eyes for a moment and tapped a pen lightly against his left temple. "*If* she wakes up."

"Yes, sir. If she wakes up."

fog

White.

The world was white.

J.D. closed her eyes. Darkness. Black.

She opened them again.

White.

She lay on her back. Sheets swaddled her, clean and crisp and white. The pillow was soft, and she shut her eyes. She was so tired, and the bed was so soft. She could drift away again. It would be easy.

But she had been asleep for so long. She felt like she had been asleep forever. It was time to wake up.

She opened her eyes to the white ceiling, the white walls. She didn't move. There was no pain. But her body felt strange — unused. New.

Maybe I can't move, she thought. The words floated across her mind, lazy and slow, the thought dripping like honey. She should probably try to move. She should sit up. She should go —

Where?

Why?

She had spent the past two weeks filled with fear, running from an enemy she couldn't see, hiding from a past she couldn't remember.

But now there was no fear.

My name is J.D., she thought. *I came here to find out who I really am. I came here to find out who's after me. I came here to fight.*

She had forgotten nothing.

"You're awake!" someone shrieked. It was a girl's voice, high and sweet.

J.D. pressed her hands flat into the mattress and pushed, trying to sit up. She shifted her weight forward, focusing on the way her elbows dug into the mattress, the way her head sank backward until she remembered to tense the muscles in her neck. She tightened her stomach muscles, drew her shoulders higher and higher.

This is how I sit up, she thought, amused, like she had learned a trick. The world dipped and lurched for a moment, then steadied. She was upright.

A girl stood in the corner of the white room, beaming.

"They said you might not wake up, but I knew you would," the girl said. She rushed over to the bed and grabbed J.D.'s hand. J.D. let her. The grip was warm, the fingers soft. J.D. smiled.

"I was so worried about you. First you disappear, then you come back, but they won't tell us anything about what happened or what's wrong, only that you —" The girl paused, nibbling at the edge of her lip. "They said you don't remember anything. That you wouldn't . . . You don't remember me, do you?"

J.D. slowly shook her head. She opened her mouth, wondering if she could speak. Her tongue felt too large. Clumsy. She ran it across her lower jaw, feeling each tooth. Some were sharp, some were smooth. How strange, how funny, she thought, that breath, tongue, and teeth somehow came together into words. She knew they did. She remembered talking. She remembered screaming.

She touched her lips, running her finger over the blistered and cracked skin.

It was so complicated. Gasping out a breath,

molding your tongue around it, opening and closing your mouth at just the right time, in just the right way. Making noises, random sounds that meant nothing unless they were in the right order.

"I'm sorry," she said. Her voice was hoarse, her throat rusty. "I don't remember you."

The girl's smile faltered, but only for a moment. Then she ran a hand through her brown hair. It was short and choppy, just like J.D.'s. "They said you wouldn't. But it's okay. You're back. You're awake. That's what matters." She handed J.D. a folded stack of clothing, all white. "This is for you, after you shower. There's a towel and shampoo and stuff in the bathroom. But you should hurry, because Dr. A. wants to see you as soon as you're ready."

"Dr. A.?"

"You don't remember him, either? Dr. Sykes?"

Ansel Sykes.

A wave of nausea washed over her, and for a moment the world seemed brighter. Sharper. *I hate him.* She clenched her muscles, ready to jump out of bed, ready to run.

Relax, something inside her commanded. *Everything*

is fine. The words felt like they were coming from somewhere else, *someone* else. But it was an order, and she obeyed.

A wave of calm washed over her, sweeping away the panic. J.D. sank backward again, back to the forgiving mattress, back to the soft pillow. Why would she run? She was safe. She was home.

"I know who he is," she told the girl. "I came here to find him." J.D. remembered walking into the LysenCorp Institute, so proud and strong, so ready to fight. She remembered facing Ansel Sykes, and the flashing lights that promised her everything would be okay. She remembered letting go of the hatred and the anger. Just . . . letting go.

He had led her down the hallway, and then — that was the last she remembered.

The girl nodded. "But how did you know to come back here, if you don't remember anything?" Then she shook her head and waved her hands. "Wait, don't tell me now, there's no time. You have to get ready. Dr. A.'s waiting. You know, he *never* meets with us one-on-one, but I guess this is a special — well, you've always been kind of . . . you know."

"What?"

"Dr. A. has no favorites," the girl said. She sounded like she was reciting from a textbook. "We are all equal in his eyes. But . . . everyone knows he likes you the best." She winked. "We always joke that that's the only reason we're best friends — you know, that I want to get in good with him."

"Best friends?" J.D. asked.

"Oh, right, you don't —" Again, the girl's smile disappeared, so quickly that J.D. almost didn't notice. And then it was back, fixed on her face like it had never gone away. "It doesn't matter. We can start fresh, right?" She held out her hand. "I'm Ilana."

"I'm J.D." J.D. shook her hand.

She'd had another best friend. Daniel.

But he had betrayed her. She had felt so alone.

None of that seemed to matter anymore.

"J.D.," Ilana repeated. "I'm so used to calling you Jordan. That is — uh, was — your name, you know. But Dr. A. says we should do whatever we can to make you feel comfortable . . . J.D." She smiled. "I can hang out here until you're ready to go see him," Ilana said. "Or I can wait outside."

J.D. shrugged. "It doesn't matter. Whatever you want."

13

Ilana reached over and gave her a hug. J.D. waited limply in her arms. Finally, Ilana stepped away and turned her back to the bed. J.D. gasped.

"Wait."

Ilana froze.

"That tattoo, on your neck — what does it mean?"

Ilana's hair was short enough that J.D could see the bare skin poking out above her white collar. There was a black mark at the base of her neck. Ilana came closer, dipping her head down so J.D. could get a better look.

"It doesn't mean anything. It's just something they gave us when we were little," Ilana said. "We all have them."

J.D. touched the back of her neck, where the LysenCorp insignia was inked into her skin, like a brand. "We?" J.D. said quietly. "So there are . . . others?"

Ilana laughed. "Lots of us. You'll meet them again soon."

"And are they . . . are you . . ."

Are you like me? she wanted to ask. *Can you move things with your mind? Have you been trained to destroy?*

But she didn't say it, just clutched the bundle of clothes to her chest. "I guess I'll shower now. So you can, uh, wait outside."

Ilana nodded and walked to the door. She raised an arm and flicked her wrist. The door flew open. She turned back and winked at J.D. "Welcome home!" The door closed behind her with another casual flick.

And for the first time since she'd opened her eyes, a real emotion — not just the memory of an emotion, not just the echo of something she used to feel — cut through her haze.

It was joy.

I'm not alone.

She stayed in the shower as long as she could, letting the steaming jets of water hammer her body. It felt good to stand; it felt good to move.

Everything felt good, she realized. For the first time in as long as she could remember, she wasn't in pain, she wasn't tired, she wasn't hungry, she wasn't scared. She just *was*. She existed, minute by minute, without care for the past or concern for the future. Life was now. And now was warm and clean and safe.

The clothes fit her perfectly. She examined her reflection in the long mirror on the inside of the bathroom door. In the white shirt, pants, and sneakers, she looked like Ilana — except that Ilana's skin was a golden olive, her hair the color of tree bark, while J.D.'s blond hair was only a few shades darker than her pale face. The clothes suited the featureless white room; they made her feel like she belonged.

She walked across the room, pausing in front of the white door. Then she raised her hand, just as Ilana had, and flicked her wrist.

Nothing happened.

I know I can do it, she thought.

She flicked her wrist again, waiting for the familiar surge of heat and power to rush through her. Nothing happened.

It's still in me, she thought. *I can find it again, if I want to.*

But there was no hurry.

A week ago, she would have tried again, tried harder. She would have been consumed by frustration and anger, and she would have used the anger as a weapon, to fight her way through the block, to regain what she had lost. But now there was no frustration, no anger, only calm.

It doesn't matter.

She twisted the doorknob and pulled. But the door didn't open. She was locked in.

J.D. shrugged. She walked back across the room, bouncing a little with each step. She liked the way her new sneakers felt against the floor, soft and springy. Then she sat down on the edge of the bed and waited. Eventually, someone would come back and tell her what to do.

The door swung open. Ilana poked her head in.

"Ready?" she asked. "They said it's time."

J.D. followed her out of the room. "How long have you lived here?" she asked as they walked down an empty white corridor.

Ilana gave her a strange look. "My whole life. We all have."

"And you . . . you like it here?"

"Of course," Ilana said. "We're all happy here. It's home."

Ilana patted her on the back. J.D. remembered that she didn't like to be touched, not by strangers.

But Ilana's hand felt warm, and the light pressure gave her comfort. *I am happy here,* she told herself. *This is home.* The words felt like her own. Like they had come from within.

The hallway dead-ended at a tall, black door. Ilana knocked.

"Is it locked?" J.D. asked.

Ilana giggled and shook her head. "Why would Dr. A. lock his door?"

"I guess you can open anything," J.D. said.

"We would *never* go where we aren't supposed to! That would be against the rules."

"Oh." That made sense, J.D. thought. It was important to follow the rules. "It's important to follow the rules," she said out loud, and the words felt as if they'd been living inside of her, waiting to rise to the surface.

Ilana nodded eagerly. "It *is*. See? Everything's starting to come back to you. And I'm sure Dr. A. will know exactly how to help, and soon you'll remember enough to —"

The door opened.

A man stood before her, his eyes hooded behind thick glasses, his bushy gray eyebrows arched, a smile playing at the corners of his lips.

J.D. jerked backward. The haze of calm suddenly lifted, and an explosion of fear and anger spewed out of her. Sykes blazed bright before her, the world around him fading to gray. Emotions churned, spinning fast and furious, terror, hate, rage, swirling together, too loud, too strong, too much. Her legs wobbled, and Ilana caught her before she could fall, before she could scream.

"It's okay," she murmured in J.D.'s ear. "It's just Dr. A."

"Let her go, Ilana," Ansel Sykes said. His voice was low and husky, a knife scraping across each word. He was holding a small gray device, his thumb hovering over one of the many buttons. "She can stand on her own."

She felt Ilana's hands fall away, and she stood on her own, facing her enemy.

Run, she thought.

Fight, she thought.

This is home, she thought. *I am happy here.*

"What happens next, J.D.?" Dr. Sykes asked, his eyes twinkling. "The decision is yours."

She didn't move.

family

"Why don't you come inside?" Dr. Sykes said, placing a hand on J.D.'s shoulder. She imagined she could feel the rough sandpaper wrinkles through the thin cloth of her shirt. "We have a lot to talk about."

When he touched her, the anger flared again. But the flame was weak, and it flickered out.

"I hate you," she said, without passion. "You're my enemy."

She felt like she was reciting a series of facts, memorized statements that had nothing to do with her. She knew what he had done to her. She knew she hated him. She just didn't *feel* it.

"Enemy? Well, let's see about that," he said, smiling. "Come on in, J.D."

And she followed him into the office. She sat down on his couch, remembering another couch, another office, when he had pretended to be her psychiatrist, pretended he wanted to help.

"I came here for answers," she said. The anger was still there, buried, and it didn't feel good. It wasn't pleasant, not like the soft bed, the clean clothes, the warm shower. It wasn't sweet and warm, like the feel of Ilana's hug or the sound of her laughter. It was an off-key note, and she wanted it to slink away, back where it came from, leave her alone. But it festered. "I want the truth."

Dr. Sykes sighed, pulling up a chair next to her. "And you deserve it. After everything you've been through, you certainly deserve that much. First of all, I apologize for the deception. It was necessary, but nonetheless, I apologize. After the explosion, when you disappeared, you have no idea how worried we all were. And when we found you again, and you'd lost your memory — well, you can understand that we had to proceed with caution, of course. I had to ascertain how much you knew, and more important, whether you still had your . . . abilities. I have to admit, I was almost hoping they'd disappeared along with your memories, and I could create a normal life for you."

"Alexa," she said. It was the identity he'd given

her, the one he'd tried to brainwash her into believing.

He hung his head. "Yes. Alexa. I merely wanted to create a happy life for you . . . but when it became clear that you'd retained more of your past than we anticipated, you needed, for your own safety, to come back here. To the Institute. I would have told you the truth about everything — but, of course, before that could happen, you ran away."

"Because you lied to me!" J.D. cried. "You told me I was crazy!"

"Again, a necessary deception." Dr. Sykes pressed the tips of his fingers together and brought them to his chin. "The truth would have been very upsetting, and I couldn't risk discussing it with you in an unprotected environment. Not after . . . the explosion."

J.D.'s eyes widened. "What do you mean?"

"Oh — you haven't figured that out by now?" Dr. Sykes said. "You must have at least suspected that you caused it. Such a horrible accident. We're just lucky no one else was hurt."

"I . . . I caused . . ." The explosion had taken down three city blocks. She had been found unconscious in the rubble. "Why would I . . . ?"

He placed a hand over hers. She didn't push it away.

"You didn't mean to, J.D. It was an accident."

She knew she had the power to do it. And in her nightmares — her memories — she'd seen herself wreak destruction. But only because *he* had made her.

"It's very important that you remember," he continued. "You are *not* a bad person. You would never willingly cause anyone pain. But . . ."

"But?"

"But accidents happen. After what happened in the barn . . . I would think you know that better than anyone."

What happened in the barn.

The woman had been chasing J.D., the woman who'd pretended to be J.D.'s mother. J.D. had been angry, and afraid, and then somehow, it had happened. Something had shot through her — shot out of her — and her mother had been thrown backward. Over a railing. Down and down and down, until she crashed with a sickening thud.

She had lain still as a fire raged around her.

And J.D. had run away.

It was just an accident, she insisted to herself. *Accidents happen.*

"You can see that girls like you, special girls, need special precautions," Dr. Sykes said. "And that's what I've created here for you. A world where you can be safe, where you can thrive, where you can learn to use your amazing gift. And where no one can take advantage of you. Because as you know, J.D., there are those out there for whom 'accidents' are a blessing. There are those who might want to use you to create more 'accidents.' Who'd want to use you to destroy."

"*You* want to use me," she said.

He frowned. "I want to *help* you."

"I don't have to believe you," she said dully. "All you do is lie to me."

"That's all in the past, J.D.," he said, standing up. "Why not let it be forgotten, like everything else you've left behind?"

He made it sound so easy.

"It's the sole purpose for this Institute, and the sole purpose of my career," he said. "To help you girls develop your gift. And J.D., of all my girls, your gift may be the most special of all."

"Special?" She twisted her mouth around the word. "I don't feel *special.* I feel like . . ."

Like a freak.

Like a monster.

"No, 'special' is exactly the right word," Ansel Sykes said eagerly. "Trust me, I've watched you girls grow up, and I know your talent can feel like a curse sometimes, but it is indeed a gift. An amazing gift."

She tried to tell herself that he could still be lying about everything. But she wanted to believe him. She wanted to believe she was special, that she wasn't a monster, designed to destroy. She wanted to believe she was just a girl, a girl with a gift.

A girl that Dr. Sykes was just trying to help.

You can trust him, the voice inside her promised. *Dr. Sykes is your friend.*

It was the same calm voice that assured her: *This is your home.*

A thick red file sat on the corner of his desk. He grabbed it and returned to J.D. "I want you to remember you're not a prisoner here. This is your home. We are your family. No more lies."

"No more lies," J.D. repeated. She sank back into the couch and rested her head against the comfy pillows. Ansel Sykes couldn't be her enemy. She felt too cozy, too safe.

He handed her the folder.

25

"What is this?" she asked, without curiosity.

"This is what you've been fighting for all this time," he said. "This is your answer, J.D. Your identity — inside that file. It's you."

"Oh." The file sat on her lap. She realized she should probably look inside. He was right: She had been waiting a long time.

She waited for him to tell her what to do.

"Go ahead," Ansel Sykes said. "Look inside."

She opened the file. The first sheet of paper was a birth certificate.

Born to
  Mother: Francine King
  Father: Peter King
  Baby girl, 6 pounds, 7 ounces
  Name: Jordan King

"They died, I'm afraid," Ansel Sykes said. "When you were three years old. That's how you ended up here, with us."

"Oh."

So her parents were dead.

"That's very sad," she said, trying to feel that it was.

She felt nothing.

"Your name is Jordan, but we're happy to call you J.D., if that's what you prefer. I know how important it is to you to hold on to that part of yourself. I know that's who you are now."

It had seemed so important. But now it just seemed silly. J.D., Jordan, what did it matter? It was just a name, just a word. Really, when you thought about it, it was just a sound, tongue and teeth and breath joining together to spill out a meaningless noise.

She paged through the rest of the folder. It was thick with memos, progress reports, photographs, all documenting the childhood of a bright, eager girl named Jordan King. "She has almost mastered the alphabet," one notation said. "Quick to make friends, eager to speak her mind," said another.

And a third: "Telekinetic abilities developing at unusual rate; advanced far beyond the other girls."

J.D.'s eyes skimmed over the reports. It was all there, the story of her life. And, although she had no memory of it, she had no doubt it was real. But it was in the past. And the past was over, just like Ansel Sykes had said.

Why not let it be forgotten, like everything else you've left behind?

She closed the file. "Done already?" he asked, sounding unsurprised.

J.D. nodded, and let him take the folder back. He slid it into a filing cabinet against the wall, then smiled at her. "Are you ready?"

"Ready for what?"

"To get back to your friends and your old life. You'd like that, wouldn't you? To get back to the way things used to be, back to normal?"

J.D. nodded again. She would like that. She would like that very much.

"Then just follow me."

She stood up and joined him by the door. He put a hand on her back and guided her into the hallway. "I've only ever wanted the best for you, J.D. I hope you understand that now."

She barely heard him. The words were just sounds. He wanted her to follow him, so she would follow him. Down one white corridor, then another, and finally, to a door labeled EXAMINATION.

"Just a few quick tests and you'll be ready to go." He stepped inside; she followed.

Part of the room was set up like a doctor's office, with a medical bed and machines and instruments scattered around the edges. The other half looked like a kindergarten classroom, with colorful blocks of all shapes and sizes stacked up against the wall. In the middle of the room, a woman on crutches stood with her back to the door. Her right leg was encased in a thick plaster cast, and gauzy white bandages covered each forearm.

"Serena, are you ready for us?" Dr. Sykes asked.

The woman turned around. J.D. gasped.

Not because of the blistering red scar running from the woman's chin to her forehead.

Not because the woman's icy blue eyes matched her own.

But because they were the eyes from her nightmares.

They were the eyes of a dead woman.

"Surprise," the woman said, twisting her mouth into a cruel smile.

They were the eyes of her mother.

alive

"I thought you were dead," J.D. whispered.

"Thought you killed me, you mean," the woman said coldly. "Disappointed?"

I'm not a murderer, J.D. thought, feeling something unclench deep inside of her. It was like she'd been holding her breath for so long she'd forgotten that it was possible to breathe. She didn't understand; it didn't make sense. She had seen the woman die, she had been so sure . . . but it didn't matter.

The woman was alive.

J.D. was not a killer.

"If you're waiting for an apology, you'll be waiting for a long time," the woman said. "I simply did what needed to be done."

J.D. felt the hate boiling inside of her, burning away the fog of contentment. *"What needed to be done?* Do you even know what you did to me? Do you know what I thought, after the barn — and you've been here, all along? You've been alive, and I almost *died* and you *did what needed to be done*?" J.D. launched herself across the room. The woman needed to understand her evil. She needed to pay. She needed to —

The light.

It blazed purple. The glow reflected off the white walls, the white ceiling, the white floors, the white clothes, filling J.D.'s field of vision, filling her brain. Purple shifted to blue, then to green, pulsing and swelling, and she could feel it on her face, soaking her skin like a ray of sun.

The light was beautiful, and she was calm and quiet and still. The light pulsed. The room glowed. J.D. floated. There was no thought. No rage, no fear, no concern. No J.D.

Only the light.

"Well, well, Ansel, it seems things aren't coming along as well as you'd led me to believe." It was the woman.

J.D. had forgotten she was in the room. She had forgotten the room, drifted away to a place without place, a time without time.

She stood still. She listened. But none of it

mattered. Only the light. It washed over the woman's face, purple, then green, then blue, beautiful.

"There are bound to be momentary setbacks," Dr. Sykes snapped. "It's immaterial. Everything's fine now. Tell her, J.D."

"Everything's fine now." It was her mouth moving, it was her voice speaking, but none of it touched her. The words belonged to someone else. Someone far away.

Dr. Sykes smiled proudly. "As you can see, she's responded quite well to treatment —"

"You can't seriously expect to keep her in this state permanently?" the woman said.

"That won't be necessary," Dr. Sykes replied. "She was doing just fine until she saw you, Serena. Which is to be expected — she believed you were dead, after all. And she's not your biggest fan."

"Nor yours," the woman pointed out.

"All a misunderstanding," Dr. Sykes said, waving his hand. "Everything's going to be alright now. J.D. just needs a little time to accommodate herself to life at the Institute and learn the rules." He turned to face J.D.

"J.D., you need to listen to me now."

The lights pulsed. She stared at his face, mesmerized by the wrinkles swirling beneath his eyes, the cavernous darkness of his mouth. She was floating, but he was calling her back.

She obeyed.

"This is Dr. Mersenne," he said. "It's very important to be polite and do as she asks, do you understand? Whatever's happened in the past, it's important to respect her. That's one of the rules here at the Institute. Do you understand?"

J.D. nodded. "It's important to follow the rules," her mouth said, and the sound of the words made her happy. She smiled.

Dr. Sykes smiled back, and that made her happy, too. "Very good. Are you ready to behave now?"

J.D. nodded. She was ready.

Dr. Sykes was holding his small gray device. He pressed a button, and the flickering, colored lights faded to white.

J.D. blinked, feeling like she'd just woken up. A warm glow radiated through her body.

"Do you remember what we just talked about?" Dr. Sykes asked.

J.D. pressed a hand to her forehead. The last few

minutes felt foggy and unclear, like everything had happened underwater. But the words came to her. "This is . . . Dr. Mersenne," she said slowly. "I'm supposed to do as she asks."

He patted her on the shoulder. "Excellent."

"But . . . I saw you fall," J.D. said. She knew she was supposed to stay calm, obey, follow the rules. She still felt the glow. But every time she looked at the woman, her muscles tensed, and everything became sharper. She felt wrong. She felt *angry*. And she knew she should look away, let herself fall back into the haze. But she didn't.

"They pulled me out after you ran away and left me to die," Dr. Mersenne said, not bothering to mask the snarl in her voice. "Only some minor burns. They tell me most will heal." She lifted a bandaged arm and traced her fingers along the blistered, blotchy red scar covering her cheek. *"Most."*

"It was an accident," Dr. Sykes said. "All is forgiven."

But J.D. kept her eyes on Dr. Mersenne and knew that nothing was forgiven. The woman glared. And despite the orders she'd been given, J.D. glared back.

"Alright," Dr. Mersenne said brusquely. "Let's get to work." She pointed to the side of the room piled with building blocks. "We'll start small, with the one-foot cubes."

J.D. didn't move.

"Well?" Dr. Mersenne asked impatiently. "Show us what you can do. Choose a cube, and lift it one foot in the air." She pulled out a stopwatch. "I'll be timing your efforts."

"You want me to *perform* for you?" J.D. asked.

Dr. Sykes cleared his throat. "J.D., we merely need to ascertain how your abilities have developed —"

"Or regressed," Dr. Mersenne added.

"Or regressed. It's just a simple series of trials. Everyone goes through it periodically. And if you want things to get back to normal, we'll need to get through this first. Those are the rules."

And it was important to follow the rules.

J.D. didn't want to perform for the woman. But she was tempted to take the stupid test, just to prove that she could. *She thinks I've got no power,* J.D. thought, keeping her eyes on Dr. Mersenne's cruel smile. *I can prove her wrong. I know it.*

She was beginning to like the way the anger made her feel; it made her feel more like herself. *What am I doing?* she thought suddenly. *Why am I going along with —*

"We're all on the same side here, J.D.," Dr. Sykes said. He stepped in front of her, blocking her view of Dr. Mersenne. She lowered her head, staring at his black loafers. She could hear the disapproval in his voice.

J.D. couldn't stop thinking about the days they'd spent together as mother and daughter, the nights J.D. had spent on the couch, cradled in the woman's arms. *She made me love her,* J.D. thought bitterly. It had all been a lie. J.D. understood that. But seeing her again, standing so close, it was hard to believe. *This is not my mother,* she reminded herself.

"Perhaps you should leave the two of us alone, Ansel," Dr. Mersenne suggested. "I'm sure J.D. and I have quite a few things to chat about."

"No!" J.D. yelped. She couldn't be left alone with the woman. Not when she was helpless and the woman had all the power. "Please, Dr. Sykes."

"Call me Dr. A.," he said. "That's what the girls call me, and I admit, I quite enjoy it."

"Dr. A., please stay."

Dr. Mersenne frowned. "Ansel, I really think you should —"

"If J.D. wants me to stay, I'll stay," he said. "But

J.D., that means you need to follow our instructions. Can you do that for me?"

She nodded.

And when Dr. Mersenne ordered her across the room toward the neat stack of blocks, she obeyed.

"This is pathetic," Dr. Mersenne snapped. "Complete regression."

J.D. stared at the small block, narrowing her eyes and trying desperately to raise it in the air, to topple it off the pile, to make it do *anything* but sit motionless, as it had for the past twenty minutes. "I can do it," she said. She told herself to stay calm, but it was so hard with Dr. Mersenne there, doubting her, feeding her hatred.

I can do it, she told herself. She had done it in the past. She just needed to remember how. It was like walking, or speaking — she just had to find the right muscles and string them together in the right order.

"How long do we have to continue this farce?" Dr. Mersenne asked. "It's obvious that whatever skills she may have had, they're gone. Perhaps if you would divulge the details of your experimental procedure, I could try to determine —"

"That's irrelevant now, Serena," Dr. Sykes said. "Let's just give her a chance."

J.D. barely heard him. She was staring at the block, wishing it into motion. But wishing wasn't enough. "I could do it before," she murmured. "I could control it."

"There's no evidence of that at all," Dr. Mersenne said. "Perhaps you deluded yourself into believing you could control it. Or perhaps you're just a liar."

"*You're* the liar!" J.D. yelled, and the red block flew across the room, right at Dr. Mersenne's head. She ducked just in time, and the wooden block smashed into a monitor screen on the opposite wall. The shower of glass sprayed across the room, and then there was silence.

"I'm sorry," J.D. said, wondering if she would be punished.

Dr. Sykes chuckled. "Don't apologize, that was excellent! Such speed, such force — I knew you had it in you. We just need to work on your control a bit. But it's clear to me that your gift is just as present — and just as strong — as ever. I'm proud of you."

He beamed at her, and J.D. blushed. She had done well. She glared at Dr. Mersenne. *I told you I could do it,* she wanted to say. *You're the liar.* I'm *special.*

But she stayed silent. *Be polite.* The thought pulsed through her. *Do as she says.*

It felt so good to be praised. It felt so good to know that someone believed in her, *wanted* her to succeed. She just had to behave.

It was important to follow the rules.

The session lasted for two hours, and by the end, J.D. had managed to lift the fifty-pound weight with her mind. But she was still unable to stack one two-pound block on top of another.

"Fine motor control is the hardest thing to achieve," Dr. Sykes said. "Brute force comes first, but I promise, soon you'll advance to the point where you can do anything."

"Soon enough?" Dr. Mersenne asked.

Dr. Sykes gave her a sharp look. "There's no timetable here. You've done really well for your first day back, J.D. Now, are you ready to rejoin your — well, they used to be your friends, and I'm sure they soon will be again."

"You want to put her back with the other girls?" Dr. Mersenne sounded incredulous. "Already? If we put her back with the others, we could pollute the whole group. We could ruin everything."

"She's not a toxin, Serena. She's just a girl."

"And you're just a fool," Dr. Mersenne snapped. "A sentimental one, if you can't see what a bad idea this is. We still don't know why she lost her memory, or whether her neurological instability is progressing. She should be sequestered in the medical wing for close supervision and further study. With me. I'll take full responsibility, and I assure you that *I* won't release her until I'm certain of her status."

J.D. hated the way they talked about her, like she wasn't even in the room. But it was important to stay calm.

"You're upsetting her, Serena. And you're beginning to upset me." He scowled, and Dr. Mersenne flinched.

But then the kind smile returned to his face. "J.D. seems perfectly healthy to me, and I think she's more than ready to get back. Home to her old bed, her old friends, her old life. Of course, it's up to her. It's up to *you*, J.D. What do you want?"

"I want . . . I want . . ."

Dr. Mersenne was hateful, her eyes stabbing. And being near her was . . . unsettling. It set J.D.'s mind racing, too fast, like she had a fever, and the thoughts leaped and danced, slipping through her fingers, and she was too slow to catch them. Life sped up, the world awoke, and it was hard. It meant anger and fear, and work. It meant fighting. And in Dr. A.'s calming presence, J.D. didn't want to fight anymore.

Outside the exam room, away from Dr. Mersenne, nothing had been clear. The world was all hazy shapes and rounded edges. Her mind was quiet and empty. Nothing mattered and all was good.

"J.D.?" Dr. Sykes prompted her. "Do you want to stay here with Dr. Mersenne, or —"

"No." She ripped her eyes away from Dr. Mersenne and focused on Dr. A., on the way his skin crinkled when he smiled.

He lied, too, she thought. *He chased me.*

But it was for my own good, she reminded herself.

"I want to go back," she said, taking a deep breath. It felt good to breathe in and out. It felt good to stand straight, her head up and shoulders back. It felt good to be healthy and strong, her power still tingling in her fingertips, a new life stretching ahead of her. "I want to go home."

doubt

"Come on, J.D., you can do it!"

J.D. cleared her mind of all thoughts. She focused on the pillow. Reached deep inside herself, and — it flew across the room and smacked into the far wall.

At least five feet off the mark.

"Good try, J.D.," Ilana said, giggling. "You're doing really well."

One of the other girls, Mara, sent her pillow across the room with the flick of a hand. It slammed squarely into the makeshift bull's-eye. "Don't listen to her," she said. "You suck. She just doesn't know it, because she sucks, too."

Ilana sank down on the edge of her bed, her lower lip wobbling.

"She's totally remedial," Mara said, laughing. Like all the girls, her hair was short and spiky. The LysenCorp tattoo at the nape of her neck poked up above the collar of her white pajamas. "But now that you're back, at least she won't be the worst one anymore."

The final girl, Katherine, took her turn. Her pillow slammed into the giant target a few inches to the left of the bull's-eye. "Don't listen to her," Katherine told J.D. "She's just mad because now that you're back, she knows she won't be anyone's favorite anymore."

"Don't be too sure," Mara said, glaring at J.D. "I doubt anyone's going to be too impressed with *that*."

J.D. sent another pillow flying across the room, and this one hit its target.

"Oof!" Mara grunted as the pillow smacked her in the face.

The girls burst into laughter. J.D. laughed hardest of all, collapsing on the bed next to Ilana — but she stopped when she saw her friend's face. "You don't suck," she whispered.

Ilana gave her a weak smile. "That's what you always say."

J.D. couldn't remember always doing anything. She didn't remember this room, with its thirteen mattresses lined up against the white walls. She didn't remember Ilana or Mara or any of the other girls. But after only a couple of hours, she already felt like she belonged. It was as if these girls already knew her — not the person she used to be, the one she could no longer remember, but *her*, now. J.D. They didn't force her to be anyone she wasn't. They didn't attack her with questions. They just welcomed her into the dorm and taught her the rules of their game, and they laughed with her and teased her, and she knew what Ansel Sykes had said was true: These girls were her friends.

They didn't ask where she'd been for the past two weeks.

J.D. hadn't asked anything, either. She hadn't asked about what it was like at the Institute, or what they thought of Dr. A., or whether they were all as happy as they seemed. Maybe because it didn't seem to matter. Why ask? She would find out for herself soon enough.

Why not just laugh and play and enjoy?

A low chime sounded, and the giggling stopped. The girls hopped off their beds and lined up, shoulder to shoulder, with their backs against the wall.

"Come on, J.D.," Ilana said. "It's time."

"Time for what?"

"Let her figure it out for herself," Mara said. "If she wants to get in trouble, that's her —"

"It's time for our medication," said a girl with red hair — J.D. thought her name was Sarit. "You have to line up to get your pill."

Don't ask questions, she thought. The voice in her head sounded sure. She asked anyway. "Medication for what? I'm not sick."

There was a long silence. The girls looked away, all except Ilana, whose face had turned pale.

"We take the medication every morning and every night," Ilana said. "It's the rule. We need it, for our own good."

"But —"

The door opened, revealing a man in a white uniform. He had a small gray rectangular device just like Dr. A.'s hanging from his waistband. And in his hands, he held a tray of small paper cups.

He held the tray out to the girl closest to the door. She took a cup, tipping it over and dumping a small yellow pill into her hand. Then she popped it into her mouth, washing it down with a drink from a second cup. She smiled. "Thank you." The man nodded, and the girl stepped away from the wall, hurrying across the room. She climbed into bed.

The man moved on to the next girl, and the next.

J.D. was the last in line, but soon the man was in

front of her. Every cup on the tray was empty, except for two. One was filled with water, the other held a yellow pill. Both cups had #13 written on them in black marker.

"Number thirteen, that's you," the man said. He kept his eyes on a spot just above J.D.'s head, as if she wasn't even there, looking back. "Remember that."

J.D. nodded her head. *Number thirteen.* Just another name.

"Take your medicine and go to bed. Dr. Mersenne's orders."

J.D. held out her hand, palm up. The man dumped the cup over and the yellow pill tumbled out. She wrapped her fist around it, then brought her hand to her mouth. He handed her the cup of water, and she drank it in one gulp.

"Very good. Dr. Sykes will be pleased to hear you're doing so well." She smiled at the man, and when he nodded, she did exactly what the other girls had done. She walked across the room to her bed. She crawled under the covers, lay on her back, and closed her eyes.

She kept them closed as the man's footsteps crossed to the door, and a moment later it clicked shut behind him.

When she opened her eyes, the room was dark.

And when she opened her fist, the little yellow pill was still there.

"I saw what you did."

The whisper floated through the dark.

J.D. turned onto her right side. Ilana was in the next bed, just a faceless outline in the night. "You shouldn't have."

"What did I do?" J.D. whispered back, wondering if anyone else was still awake.

"You didn't take your pill."

"Are you going to tell?" J.D. whispered.

There was a long pause. "I should. It's against the rules . . . but you're my best friend."

My best friend, J.D. thought. The words conjured up a face in her mind. Daniel.

"You have to take the pills," Ilana whispered.

"I know. It's important to follow the rules." But this time, the words sounded a little hollow.

"Not just that. We *need* them. They keep us . . . you can't tell anyone that I told you this, okay?"

"Okay."

"What we do, the telekinesis? Our brains aren't made for it. They can get messed up, like, um, when you plug in too much and you blow a fuse. The pills, they keep the circuit working. They keep us from, um . . ."

"Blowing a fuse?"

"You have to take them," Ilana urged her.

"How do you know?"

Ilana didn't answer, and the silence stretched on so long that J.D. thought she had fallen asleep.

"I've been having these dreams," Ilana whispered suddenly.

"Everyone has dreams."

"Mine, um, happen when I'm awake," Ilana admitted. "And sometimes I hear things that aren't there. Or I remember things that didn't happen. And sometimes I just, um, I can't remember things that did."

J.D. knew how that felt. It happened to her, too. All of it. But she didn't say anything.

"Dr. A., he, uh, he told me about the brain thing. He's afraid . . . I mean, he didn't say it, but I could tell, he thinks . . ."

"What?"

"What Mara said before?" Ilana whispered. "That I suck?"

"She's just a —"

"No, it's true. I'm weak. Everyone knows it. And

Dr. A. says it's not my fault, but that maybe my brain just isn't wired to . . . anyway, he said it would be okay. He promised. And he changed my, uh, dosage. In my pill. He said that would fix it. But . . ." She sighed softly. "It still happens. The dreams."

J.D. stretched her hand under her pillow, wrapping her fingers around the yellow pill. But then she let go, leaving it where it was.

"You'll be fine," J.D. whispered. "Everything will be okay."

"I know," Ilana agreed. "Everything is always okay."

J.D. closed her eyes.

The room was filled with the sounds of sleep — rhythmic breathing, rustling sheets, light snoring, and every few minutes, a deep sigh. She liked how it felt, lying there surrounded by friends. Listening to them in the dark made her feel safe. Protected. It reminded her that she wasn't alone.

Strange, how two places could be so similar, and yet so different. There had been a room full of beds at the Chester Center for Juvenile Services, where she'd spent two long nights after the explosion. There had been a row of girls all sleeping in the same uniform, all breathing in and out in the dark-ness. Just like this — and yet so different. That room had been cold, the beds hard, the sheets too rough and too thin. And J.D. had felt surrounded by enemies, alone in the world.

Alone except for Daniel.

He was back there now, at the Center, the place he hated most in the world. J.D. wondered what he would think if he could see her. Something told her he wouldn't approve.

Daniel didn't like to behave; he didn't believe in rules. He didn't know how to trust. He wouldn't get why she did.

He's not like me, she thought. *He wouldn't understand.*

He would want to know why she hadn't asked more questions. He would wonder why she believed everything she was told, and why she no longer wanted to fight. He had fought so hard for her. He had risked everything.

And now she had given up.

I'm not breaking the rules, she thought, creeping through the dark halls. *No one said I couldn't leave the dormitory. No one said I couldn't explore.*

She padded barefoot down the corridor, her way

lit by dim fluorescent panels along the wall. There were several locked doors blocking off the corridors, but that was no problem for J.D. She smiled as she forced one open with her mind. She was getting stronger. Sykes's office was where she remembered it. Inside there would be a filing cabinet, the one that held the facts of her life, and who knew what else? She would just look around, she told herself. She just needed to confirm that Dr. A. was telling the truth, and that the Institute was everything he said it was. Then she would sleep.

This is not against the rules, she told herself, putting her hand on the door. And somehow that thought made it easier to twist the knob.

The door swung open. She gasped.

"Come on in, J.D." Ansel Sykes was standing behind his desk. "I was almost afraid you weren't coming."

accident

"Sit down, sit down." Dr. Sykes gestured to one of the chairs across from him. J.D. sat. "Officially, I'm very disappointed," he said sternly. "You're not supposed to be out of your room after lights-out. Unofficially?" He sighed. "I probably shouldn't admit this, but I would have been more disappointed if you hadn't shown up."

"But how did you know I would?"

"Oh, J.D. You were always the most curious, always asking questions, so eager to test your boundaries. And I'm glad to see that hasn't changed. It would have been easier for everyone if you'd trusted me immediately, without question, but then . . . then you wouldn't have been you, am I right?"

"I trust you," she protested.

He rested his hands on the desk, folding his fingers together, and leaned toward her. "If that were true, you would have taken your medication, now wouldn't you?"

"I —"

"Don't lie to me."

J.D. slumped in the chair. "How did you know?"

"I keep telling you, J.D. I know you." He sighed. "It's crucial that you take the medication. Not that there's anything for you to worry about, but you have to remember that your gift doesn't come without strings attached. There are certain . . . considerations to keep in mind. I hope I'm not scaring you?"

I already know, J.D. wanted to say. *I know what the pills are for.* But she wouldn't betray Ilana.

"The human brain has great untapped capacity," Sykes said. "But it also has certain limitations, and while it's our job to *push* those limitations, we must be careful not to push too far. The medication will help with that. It's for your own good. But as I say, I know you, J.D., and I know you've got no reason to believe me. Not when all I've given you are half-truths." He lifted a file off his desk. It was the red file he'd shown her earlier, the one that told the story of her life. He handed it to her. "I'd hoped to spare you this, but now I see that's not possible."

J.D. didn't understand. "I've already seen all this," she reminded him. "I know who I am now."

"You don't know everything," he said. "Not yet. Go on, open it."

A news clipping lay on top, one she hadn't seen before.

Roof Collapse Kills Two, Toddler Survives

A local couple died today when their roof collapsed without warning. Their three-year-old daughter escaped with only minor injuries. Policemen on the scene ruled the tragedy a "freak accident," unable to explain how the roof, which showed no serious structural flaws, could have suddenly fallen in. It took rescue crews more than four hours to unearth the victims. Peter and Francine King, both age 34, were pronounced dead on the scene. The county medical examiner confirmed that Mr. King died instantly, from a blow to the head, while Ms. King is believed to have been crushed by the heavy rubble.

"It wasn't your fault," Dr. Sykes said. He had come out from behind his desk and was standing beside her, reading over her shoulder. "It's important that you remember that. You were just a child, so young. You would never have . . ."

J.D. put the file back on the desk and realized her hands were shaking. She stood up and faced Ansel Sykes. "What are you saying?"

"You didn't mean for it to happen," he said. "And you can't allow yourself to be dragged down by guilt."

"What are you saying?" she repeated, trying to keep her voice from breaking.

"It was a temper tantrum," he said quietly. "Or so I gather. You were just a toddler having a temper tantrum, like any normal child would. Except, of course, you were no normal child."

J.D. backed away from him, bumping against the desk. She shook her head. "No. *No.* I didn't. I couldn't."

Mr. King died instantly, from a blow to the head.

Ms. King is believed to have been crushed by the heavy rubble.

"You *did*, J.D." He took a step toward her, trapping her against the desk. "You can and you did, and it's important to understand that. We can't go forward until you accept the truth. The *whole* truth."

"It was an accident," she said, blinking. The world

went blurry, and then her cheeks were wet. She ignored the tears. "It says right here, a 'freak accident.'"

"It was an accident, yes. Investigators were mystified — a solid roof, a structurally sound house, such things don't just happen. They couldn't have known. But I keep my eyes open. As soon as I saw the reports, I knew. And I think, if you look inside yourself, you'll have to admit: You know, too."

"No." She shook her head, shook her whole body. "No!"

"Yes." He put his hands on her arms and gripped tight. *"Yes."*

No. It wasn't possible. It couldn't be possible. He had to be lying and he needed to stop. She had to make him stop. He kept gripping her, kept shaking her, and his mouth was moving but she couldn't make out the words because she was too angry. She was so angry, and tears blinded her vision and deep within the anger burned hot and the fire washed over her body and she would make him stop talking, she would make him stop lying, she would make him *stop*!

His grip slipped from her arms as his body flew across the room. It was as if a giant hand had lifted him up and flung him against the far wall. He slammed into the filing cabinets with a deafening clang, his head cracking sharply against the metal.

He didn't move.

"I didn't mean to," J.D. whispered. She realized her fists were clenched and opened them up, wiping her sweaty palms against her pajamas. "What did I do, what did I do, what did I do . . . ?"

Ansel Sykes moaned.

He was alive.

She took one step toward him, then another. And then she froze, afraid to get any closer. Afraid to see what she had done.

He sat up gingerly, propping his back against the filing cabinets. He blinked slowly, once, twice, and then rubbed the back of his head, wincing. "Can you help me up?" he asked, holding his arms up toward J.D.

She didn't move. "I can't," she whispered, trembling all over. "What if . . . what if I do it again?"

She could have killed him. Without meaning to, without wanting to, she could have killed. And it wouldn't have been the first time.

Mr. King died instantly, from a blow to the head.

Ms. King is believed to have been crushed by the heavy rubble.

She was too old for temper tantrums now. She was too powerful.

"You won't do it again, J.D. It's alright. Everything's alright now." He smiled. But then he rubbed his shoulder, the shoulder that had smashed into the metal cabinet. And her tears started to flow. "J.D.," he said, softly but firmly. "It's alright. Give me your hands."

She forced herself to go to him. She grabbed his hands and pulled him to his feet. "I'm sorry," she said, almost without sound. She stared at the plush white carpeting.

"You didn't mean to," he assured her.

But that was the problem. "I'm out of control. I'm —" Her voice broke, and she blinked back more tears, wiping a hand against her dripping nose. "I'm dangerous."

"J.D., look at me."

She shook her head, still staring at the ground.

"Look at me."

She didn't want to, but after what had just happened, she owed him. She had to listen.

Slowly, her chin rose, and their eyes met.

"You *are* dangerous," he said. "I'm not going to lie to you, not again. You have to know what's at stake here."

She almost wished he *had* lied to her; the truth hurt too much.

"*But.* You're also strong, and you can handle this. I know you, J.D. You can handle anything . . . with my help. The pills you take are a part of that. They help you stay calm and avoid emotional outbursts, the kind that can be dangerous . . . as you've seen. And if you give me the chance, I can teach you how to prevent any further 'accidents.' I can teach you to control yourself."

"But what if you can't?" she asked. "What if this, this *thing* inside of me is too strong, and —"

"You're stronger, J.D. But the problem is, you're not as strong as you think you are — not yet. You like to do things on your own, I know that. But you can't do this on your own. You can't be too strong to listen to me and accept my help. And with my help, you will tame it, just like the other girls have. Do you believe me?"

She *wanted* to believe him. But what if he was wrong?

"How?" she asked. "How can you . . . fix me?"

"Over the years, I've developed a series of techniques for helping you curb your impulses — and, occasionally, constraining them when they prove too strong for you to handle. Some of this may seem unorthodox to you."

"The lights," she said, remembering how the flashing lights had made her feel, the glorious sense of calm and contentment.

"Yes, very good." He nodded. "That's proven to be one of our most effective and humane techniques. And of course, it's all intended to help you. Help you in a way that the outside world could never understand. If you were left out there, well, all it would take was one temper tantrum, and . . ." He nodded toward the red folder. "Out there, things happen, accidents happen. And it's not a very understanding world."

She got his meaning.

Out there, she was dangerous — she had killed. Without someone to help her, without someone to *teach* her, she could kill again. And not everyone would believe it had been an accident.

"But here at the Institute, we give you the tools you need to cope with your abilities, to rein them in, so that accidents need never happen again. The medication is just one crucial part of that. Everything we do here has the same purpose: to protect you."

"Why?" she asked.

"Why what?"

"Why do all this? Take us in. Protect us."

He sighed. "I'll admit, I'm a scientist, and at first, I saw you girls as fascinating puzzles, keys to a mystery I'd been investigating for most of my career. I monitored orphanages and foster homes and found girls who fit the profile, girls who had nowhere else to go — always girls, for some reason. The telekinetic gene sequence doesn't appear in boys. I brought all of you in so I could study you. So that I could learn how it is your brains have unlocked their hidden potential."

Study me, she thought. *Like a science project. Like a lab rat.*

"But that was only the beginning," he said quickly. "As soon as I got to know you girls — and you were all just children then, children with no homes, no parents, no one to protect and care for you, except for me. It's no longer just about science. It hasn't been, for a long time. It's about you, now. My girls. You depend on me, and I can't turn my back on you. I won't. And I promise you, J.D., now that you're back, now that you're safe, we'll get through this. Together. But only if you cooperate. Only if you can bring yourself to trust me."

"I'm sorry," she said again, not knowing quite what she was apologizing for, or to whom. "I'm so sorry."

"Don't apologize," he said. "Just let me help you. Let us all help you."

"What if I'm not as strong as you think I am?" she asked quietly.

"You need only be strong enough to give in." He hugged her, cradling her against his chest. "True strength right now means accepting that you're not on your own anymore. Admit you need help, and trust me enough to supply it."

She pressed her cheek to his shirt and closed her eyes.

Dr. Sykes walked her back to the dormitory, pausing in front of the door. "I'm glad you came to me tonight, J.D. I hope you'll always come to me when you have questions or doubts. But next time, let's do it in the daytime, okay? I'm an old man, I need my beauty sleep."

J.D. laughed, wondering how she could have once

thought this man was her enemy. What might have happened to her out in the world if he hadn't been watching, if he hadn't acted to protect her? She didn't want to think about it. "Okay."

He patted her on the shoulder and pulled open the door. "Sleep well," he said. "Tomorrow, we make a fresh start."

The door closed behind her, sealing her in the darkness. She tiptoed across the room, completely blind, feeling her way from bed to bed until she reached the one at the end of the wall. *My bed*, she thought.

She'd never had a real identity or a real home, so she'd never had anything of her own. Not until now. But this bed was hers, just like this place was hers. And huddled beneath the covers, her eyes squeezed shut, it was almost possible to forget what she had learned — and what she had done.

Almost, but not quite.

When she closed her eyes, she tried to call up their faces, Francine and Peter King. She imagined the horror in their eyes as they stared down at their angry toddler, pulling down the roof with her mind. For so long, J.D. had struggled to remember who she was. Now that she finally knew, it would have been so much easier to forget.

But I can't forget, she told herself. Knowing what she was capable of gave her a purpose; it gave her a reason to change.

J.D. reached her hand under her pillow and closed her fingers around something tiny and hard, rolling it between her fingertips. Then she opened her mouth and placed it on her tongue. The pill was bitter, and she swallowed hard, nearly choking as it scraped down her throat. Then she closed her eyes, imagining the little yellow pill dissolving within her, drifting through her system, coating her insides, seeping through her blood, and healing her brain.

She felt better already.

breakdown

Every day was the same. And every day was good.

For the first time, there were no questions. There was no doubt. There was no fear. There was only the Institute, the daily routine, the following instructions and obeying the rules.

And that was good, too. Because the instructions made life easy, and the rules made it orderly. There was no need to think and no cause to fight.

One day passed, then two, and then she stopped counting. There was no need.

Every day was the same, and it began with a pill.

The girls were awoken at dawn, or so they were told. In a windowless room in a windowless building, it could have been noon, it could have been night. But they were told it was dawn, and so it was.

The pills arrived with water. J.D. always received hers last, and she always swallowed it. The taste was always bitter, and that made her happy, because bitterness meant it was strong. It was working.

They ate breakfast in a small cafeteria, and they ate in silence.

In the dormitory, on their own, they talked. They laughed, they played, they smiled. But in the halls, in the classroom, in the cafeteria, they sat quietly, they watched their hands, and they behaved. No one needed to tell J.D. the rule. She watched, and she understood. There was no reason to question it: This was the way things were. This was Dr. A.'s way, which meant it was the right way.

The workers wore white and didn't speak to the girls. They would speak if someone broke a rule. But no one ever did.

Only the teachers spoke, interchangeable men and women in white uniforms who never smiled. The girls sat motionless, staring at lead weights and raising them from floor to ceiling. They snapped steel rods, broke locks, smashed glass, tore through make-shift walls, all with their minds.

It was difficult, at first, channeling the tingling heat that coursed through her into a single motion. She struggled to do the simplest tasks, the ones the other girls had no trouble with. She tried to ignore Mara's knowing smirks when she fumbled a dexterity task or when the weights she was lifting crashed to the floor. The power was within her, she could feel it. But forcing it into a narrow beam, taming it to obey commands? That was different. That was hard.

Hard but not frustrating. Even Mara's smirks and muttered insults couldn't discourage her. The training would come back to her eventually. She would learn, she would progress, all in time. There was no cause for frustration. She need only listen, and learn, and wait.

So Dr. A. said.

She met with him every day. The other girls never did.

Every afternoon, the other girls filed down a hallway and disappeared around a corner for advanced lessons. J.D. joined Dr. A. in the greenhouse.

Mara said it was because she was remedial. But Mara was just jealous.

They sat in the greenhouse, drinking milk and sharing a plate of Oreos. It was a beautiful, peaceful space, bordered on all sides by a neat row of trees. The pink and purple flowers bloomed bright, safe from the winter cold. And J.D. and Dr. Sykes huddled over a small table amid the lush green, warmed by the pale December sun.

Afterward, J.D. could never remember what they had talked about, but that didn't matter. What mattered was that Dr. A. took time every day to see her, because he cared about her progress — and because, as he said, she was special.

None of the girls would speak about their advanced lessons, not even Ilana, and so J.D. never spoke about her meetings with Dr. Sykes. She tried not to let it bother her that her new friends went off without her every day, that they shared a secret and she was shut out.

She would join them soon, Dr. A. promised her. Overexertion was dangerous. Patience was necessary.

When the girls returned to the dormitory from their advanced session, J.D. tried not to care where they had been or what they had done. She tried not to care that they wouldn't tell her. She wasn't jealous.

They were the ones who should have been jealous.

Because she was special.

Every day was the same, and every night was the same.

Before, in the outside world, she had slept in fear, chased by her past. She had dreamed of explosions, fire, pain, and death.

Now she dreamed only of the hallway.

It was white, like all of the Institute's hallways.

It led to a red door. She had never seen a red door in the Institute, but in the dream, it seemed familiar. A sweet and somber melody played in her head.

She walked down the hallway, the men in white following closely behind.

The letters on the door read ENCODING. And even before it opened, she knew: Ansel Sykes waited inside.

No one spoke.

Dr. Sykes stood next to a chair, and she knew it was her chair, and so she sat down. The metal was cool to the touch, but the straps that wrapped around her wrists and neck were warm. The melody played on.

Dr. Sykes held a syringe of green liquid, and she knew it would burn. But the straps held her down, and the needle slipped into her skin, and the liquid ran through her veins.

And then, always, she woke up.

Lying there in the dark of night, listening to the other girls breathe, she would remember an image, a sound, even a word from the dream, and she would feel a twinge of fear. She would wonder what it meant. Feeling silly, she would trace her fingers along her arm, picturing a needle sliding in, imagining she could feel a mark.

But sleep always arrived. And in the morning, there was noise and light and laughter, and then it was time for medication.

After that, the fear was gone.

Every day was the same, but free time never got boring, because there was so little of it. Every afternoon before dinner, the door to the dormitory closed behind them, and the girls were on their own. They made up their own games, they gossiped, they joked, and sometimes they even argued, although this was rare. Argument was discouraged.

On the day everything changed, J.D. sat in a corner of the room next to Ilana. Her best friend. They sat with their legs crossed and their backs to the wall, competing to see who could hold a sneaker in the air longer. J.D. always won; Ilana never seemed to mind.

"Can I ask you something?" J.D. asked when her sneaker finally tumbled to the ground.

Ilana brushed a hand through her hair. "Sure," she said softly.

With every day that passed, Ilana's voice got softer and her smile got smaller. The night before, after lights-out, she had confided to J.D. that her headaches were getting worse. Her dreams — the ones that came over her during the day — had grown more vivid. Sometimes, she admitted quietly, she was afraid she might not wake up.

J.D. told her not to worry.

"What do you do in those advanced lessons?" J.D. asked. "When I go off to meet with Dr. A., what do you guys do?"

Ilana shrugged. "I told you before, we train. You know. Learn how to do stuff better."

"But what kind of stuff?" J.D. asked. She didn't know why it was important to her, but she felt she had to know.

Ilana winced, and rubbed the side of her head. "Just *stuff*."

"Why does it have to be this big secret?" J.D. asked. "I thought we were best friends."

"We are!"

"So come on," J.D. pressed. "Just tell me."

"I told you," Ilana said. "It's nothing. We just, you know."

"I *don't* know."

"They teach us. We do exercises. We learn." Ilana pressed both hands to her forehead. "Do we have to talk about this? I have a headache."

"Fine. We don't have to talk at all," J.D. snapped.

Ilana flinched. "I'm sorry, I don't know what you want me to say."

J.D. never spoke to her like that. She never spoke to anyone like that, not at the Institute. And J.D. knew she should apologize. But she didn't. "I just want you to tell me what happens when I'm not there."

"I told you."

"Tell me more," J.D. insisted. She felt like a bully and knew that had to be against the rules. But she had to know.

"I don't . . . we just have lessons. They're fun, and we learn new stuff. I . . . I don't remember more than that," Ilana whispered.

"You don't have to lie to me," J.D. said, feeling a strange emotion. It took her a moment to recognize it: anger. "If you're refusing to tell me, just admit it."

"I can't — I can't talk about this anymore," Ilana said, covering her face with her hands. "My head . . . I just need . . . I have to lie down."

J.D. didn't know whether Ilana was really in pain or whether it was just another lie to make J.D. stop asking questions. Or maybe to make J.D. feel sorry for her. Either way, the conversation was over. J.D. stood up and joined the rest of the girls on the other side of the room, where Mara was telling a long and confusing joke. It wasn't funny, but when the other girls laughed, J.D. did, too. And she was careful not to let her eyes stray across the room, where Ilana had crawled into bed and hidden her head under a pillow.

Best friends don't keep secrets, she thought.

But maybe she was wrong.

She'd only had one other friend, and hadn't she kept secrets from him?

J.D. decided to apologize. She didn't even know why she'd started the fight, and it wasn't worth losing a friend. She slipped out of the dormitory into the bathroom next door — it was the only place the

73

girls were allowed to go on their own. Above the sink, a large dispenser spit out paper cups. J.D. grabbed one and filled it with water. She would bring it to Ilana — water always helped her headaches — and she would fix things.

She heard the screams as soon as she stepped back into the hallway. They got louder when she opened the door to the dormitory.

Ilana stood in the middle of the room, her eyes wide, her arms splayed out at her sides. The other girls formed a horrified ring around her.

"No! No!" Ilana cried. "You can't, it burns, please, no, don't!" She shook her head violently, then flung out an arm. A nightstand flew across the room, and the girls shrieked and ducked out of the way. J.D. stood frozen in the doorway.

"I can't do that, don't make me do that!" Ilana whimpered. "No, his face, I saw his face, he was smiling, and oh, there's blood on me please please no I can't he's dead he's dead can't you see he's dead, what did I do?"

And then J.D. was knocked out of the way as two men in white barreled into the room. One of them grabbed Ilana from behind, pinning her arms to her sides. The other pulled a gray device from his belt and pressed a button near the top.

Ilana screamed.

The blood drained out of her face. She flung her head back and let out a wordless howl, like an animal. J.D. turned her face away. She couldn't stand to watch.

But she couldn't close her ears, and she couldn't block out the screams. And then, as suddenly as it had begun, it stopped.

Ilana hung limp in the man's arms. He scooped her up and strode out of the room. The second man followed, pausing in the doorway to address the girls. "Someone will come for you soon. Don't move, and don't worry. Everything will be fine."

The door closed. J.D. realized her arm was wet, and there was a small puddle on the floor by her feet. She had squeezed her hand into a fist, crushing Ilana's cup of water.

Then she realized her cheeks were wet, too.

But the man had said not to worry. She tried her best.

punished

"Ilana suffered a minor medical episode and has been taken to the infirmary," Dr. Mersenne announced. The girls were seated before her in two orderly rows. "This is nothing you need to worry about. However, we do want to run some standard tests on each of you, to make sure no one else is at risk. So when I call your name —"

"At risk for what?" J.D. called out, then snapped her mouth shut in surprise. She hadn't meant to interrupt. That was against the rules. But she couldn't focus on the rules, not after what had happened to Ilana . . . whatever it was.

"Did I say you could ask a question?" Dr. Mersenne said, glaring.

The other girls looked at J.D. in shock. No one questioned the doctors. Maybe they were wondering if this is how it began with Ilana; if she would be next.

Her head was cloudy and confused with too much emotion, and J.D. wondered if they were right.

"She was weak and she cracked," Mara said, glaring at J.D. "She was always weak. Just like you."

"That's enough." Dr. Mersenne nodded at the two men standing by the door. They walked quickly to J.D.'s seat, standing one on either side. "Mara has a point — you are our most . . . *delicate* student." Her lips curled in disgust. "Perhaps it would be expedient to begin with you. Follow me."

J.D. stood up and followed her into a small examining room. *I don't want to go with her,* she thought, and was confused by her own reaction. It wasn't a matter of what she wanted. She'd been given an order; she obeyed. That's how it worked. But imagining being trapped in the small room with Dr. Mersenne, she felt a sudden urge to flee.

Two guards stood behind her, blocking the exit.

"You may leave," the doctor told them.

One of the men shook his head. "We've been told to stay with her. *He's* concerned."

Dr. Mersenne sighed and turned to J.D. "Just lie

down on the examining table, and let's get this over with."

"No."

Dr. Mersenne looked like she couldn't believe what she'd heard. J.D. could barely believe she'd said it. It was Ilana. Since it had happened, since J.D. had heard those screams, she'd been feeling strange. Upset and angry and, for the first time in days, afraid. Being near Dr. Mersenne didn't help. Being around her made the old feelings bubble up. Staring at Dr. Mersenne, looking into those cold blue eyes, J.D. forgot everything. Everything except for the rage.

"Not until you tell me what happened to Ilana," she insisted.

Dr. Mersenne shrugged. "Everyone's brain is different. Some are strong enough to fight. Some are weak and easily controlled. Some are just broken." She smiled coolly. "Would you like to hear which of those options describes you?"

J.D. balled her hands into fists. "I don't need you to tell me who I am."

Dr. Mersenne laughed. "Of course you do. Me, or someone like me. That's who you are, *J.D.* Just an empty sieve waiting to be filled. Always looking for someone to tell you what to do."

"I am not!" J.D. shouted. The rage rose within her; it was like an old friend.

One of the men took a step forward. "Doctor, maybe you should —"

"I'm handling this," Dr. Mersenne said, holding up a hand to stop him. "Nothing to worry about here. Not from this one."

J.D. realized she was being dismissed.

"I want to see her," J.D. said. "Ilana."

"That's not going to happen."

"I'm not leaving until you let me see her."

"She's gone," Dr. Mersenne said. "And she's not coming back, so you might as well forget about her. Let it go, J.D. You're so good at that, after all. Moving on. *Forgetting.*"

J.D. took a deep breath. She focused, sinking into herself, blocking everything out but the exam table. Four legs and a metal slab.

It took barely any mental effort to throw it across the room. It crashed against a wall and clattered to the floor.

Dr. Mersenne was smiling.

"You see what I can do!" J.D. screamed. "Now take me to see —"

She gasped and doubled over.

Pain.

Pain like nothing she had ever felt.

It sizzled inside of her. She felt like her blood was boiling. She felt like something was ripping her inside out. *What's happening?* she had time to think, and then the pain swelled and a red mist exploded in her mind and she thought nothing.

She heard Dr. Mersenne shouting, but the words were just noise.

She heard a scream, like an animal, like Ilana, and it went on and on, echoing, rising and falling, and it was her voice, her scream, her pain.

She was on the floor. She was staring at the ceiling, writhing, still screaming, and it wouldn't end and the woman was still shouting and a man burst into the room and she screamed and screamed and then the pain stole her breath and she gasped for air and the world faded into gray.

Something clattered to the floor.

And the pain was gone.

J.D. lay on her back with her eyes closed, taking slow, deep breaths, waiting.

She waited for the pain to return.

And she knew if it did, this time, she wouldn't survive.

"What's going on here?" It was Ansel Sykes's voice, and it was angry.

"Ask *him*." That was Dr. Mersenne.

"The situation was escalating," the guard's voice said, "and she refused to take measures, so I was forced to —"

"You were strictly instructed to refrain from disciplinary measures unless there was absolutely no other option," Sykes shouted.

"I had to," the guard protested. "I thought she was going to —"

"Return to your quarters," Sykes said very quietly. "I'll be there soon to deal with you."

Footsteps, and then a door closed.

J.D. opened her eyes just enough to let in a slit of light. A small gray device lay on the floor next to her; it was the same device that everyone on the staff carried. A moment later, a hand reached down to pick it up. And then someone touched her shoulder. She whimpered, expecting more pain, but there was nothing. Her body felt normal, and the pain was gone.

Except it still blazed through her mind.

"Better now?" Dr. Sykes asked gently.

He had carried her to his office and laid her down on the couch. She watched him through slitted eyes as he dropped the device into a desk drawer. Then he sat down next to her, waiting.

"I think it's time to sit up, don't you?" he said finally, obviously aware she wasn't asleep.

J.D. opened her eyes and gingerly pushed herself upright. Nothing hurt, and already the memory of the pain was beginning to fade. But the fear was louder than ever, pulsing with every thump of her heartbeat. "What happened?"

Dr. Sykes shook his head. "I explained to you before about the need for certain . . . unorthodox disciplinary measures, for extreme circumstances only. I'm afraid a member of the staff got a little overanxious. I can't apologize enough, but I assure you, he *will* be dealt with."

"It was Dr. Mersenne," J.D. said.

"No. Just one of the staff."

"No, it was *her*, she hates me!" J.D. insisted.

"Dr. Mersenne is a professional," he argued. "And it's her job to keep you healthy."

"When she looks at me, I can tell she —"

"Dr. Mersenne is not a warm person," Dr. Sykes said. "She's a brilliant scientist, and very committed to her work, but she's never been what you would call . . . comfortable around children. I know she put on a very compelling act for you while you were living as mother and daughter —"

"I don't want to talk about that," J.D. muttered. She refused to remember a time when she'd thought Dr. Mersenne loved her, when she'd let that woman hug her and whisper lying terms of endearment.

"I would just hate to think you were expecting something from her that she can't deliver."

J.D. gritted her teeth. "I'm not expecting anything. Not from her."

"For Dr. Mersenne, this is a job. A job she's passionate about and committed to, but a job nonetheless." He rested his hand on J.D.'s for just a moment, then took it away again. "I hope you understand it's not the case for all of us — but it is for her. That said, it's her job to monitor your progress and make sure you stay healthy. That's all she was trying to do."

J.D. tugged at the edge of her sleeve, wrapping it around her fingers. "What happened to Ilana?" she asked, without meeting his eyes.

"Ilana is gone. She's no longer your concern."

It was the answer she'd been expecting, but it still made her chest tighten. "But what happened to her?"

Dr. Sykes sighed. "I've explained to you that telekinetic brains are prone to certain neural instabilities — it's why I've been so concerned about you pushing yourself too far, too fast. And of course, why it's so important that you continue with your medication to regulate your brain activity. But Ilana . . . well, certain brains are inherently unstable. We did everything we could to keep this moment from arriving, but I'm afraid we failed."

"So you're saying her brain just . . . broke?" J.D. touched the side of her head lightly, like it was fragile. Which maybe it was.

"That's one way of putting it. You can think of your brain as a large circuit board, and all your thoughts and feelings as electrical impulses. Ilana's brain had a bit of a . . . power surge, and some of her circuits seem to have blown out."

"So how long will it take you to fix her?"

Dr. Sykes didn't answer. He just looked at J.D. with a strange expression, not quite sad, more like . . . disappointed. Like she had somehow failed by asking the question. Like she should already have known the answer.

"You *can* fix her, right?" J.D. asked. "You have to."

Dr. Sykes pulled a white handkerchief out of his pocket and handed it to her. She realized her eyes were leaking. He held out a pill.

"Take this," he urged her. "You'll feel better. Remember, it's important to stay calm and keep yourself under control."

J.D. knew she should take the pill. It was wrong to cry, just as it was wrong to shout and wrong to scream and wrong to fight. It was right to forget and move on, and even in a few short days, she'd become an expert at both.

You're good at forgetting. The memory of Dr. Mersenne's voice taunted her. J.D. stiffened. She didn't want to forget Ilana, and she didn't want to forget the pain.

Dr. A. is on my side, she thought. "I'm fine," she said, wiping away her tears.

But Dr. Sykes still held out the pill, nodding at her. It was a silent command, and she obeyed, taking the pill from his open palm and slipping it into her mouth. She lodged it under her tongue and forced her face into a placid smile. "Everything is alright."

To her own ears, she sounded like a robot. But Dr. Sykes grinned. "That's my girl. Ready to go off and join your friends at dinner?"

"If you want me to," she said, knowing it was the right answer.

He patted her back. "Yes, I do. That is exactly what I want."

As soon as the door closed behind her, she spit out the pill and stepped on it, grinding it into a pile of fine dust.

Why did I just do that? she thought in horror. If Dr. A. thought she should take a pill, then she should take it. He knew best, and it was best for her to stay calm. To forget Ilana, to forget the pain. But she didn't want to forget.

Remember, she told herself over and over again. The word helped keep her head clear.

Dinner had started twenty minutes before, and the other girls were all seated, silently chewing their food. J.D. went through the small cafeteria line on her own. She collected her tray and her drink and stared down at her plate as someone slopped a scoop of mashed potatoes onto it. She didn't want anyone to see how red and watery her eyes were.

"Are you okay?" the worker whispered.

J.D. flinched. Staff never spoke to the girls — she must have looked even worse than she'd thought. She nodded quickly, gripping the edges of her tray and never taking her eyes off the plate.

"So you ready to get out of here?" he whispered. "I've got a plan."

She looked up.

The tray fell to the floor. Her glass shattered, and a sticky mud of soda and mashed potatoes pooled at her feet. J.D. couldn't breathe.

The boy behind the counter still held a slab of chicken between his tongs, ready to deposit it on her plate. He winked. She wheezed.

The world had slipped into slow motion, but then she opened her mouth and time jolted forward again. She could speak.

"Daniel?"

reunion

"What are you doing here?" she whispered as he hurried around the counter with a mop and began cleaning up her spill. He was pretending not to look at her.

"What do you think I'm doing?" he said out of the side of his mouth. "I'm here to rescue you."

J.D. knelt down and began carefully picking up the larger pieces of glass, collecting them in a thick napkin. "I don't need rescuing," she whispered. "I don't need *you*. This is my home."

"J.D., I told you, I didn't mean to turn you in, I was just worried —"

"I'm not mad," she said. "I'm not anything. But you shouldn't be here. I belong here. You don't."

"Belong here?" He looked at her like she was crazy. "J.D., *Sykes* is running this place. Your mortal enemy, remember?"

She shook her head. "Dr. Sykes is on my side. Everything is alright."

"No one's listening, you don't have to pretend. I know you're playing along, and that's why you ignore me every time I pass you in the halls —"

"I'm not ignoring you," she protested. "This is the first time I've seen you here."

"First time? You've seen me every day, you just pretend I'm not there, and —"

"What's going on here?" a woman said sternly, pulling Daniel's mop out of his hands. "You know the rules." She turned to J.D. "Is he bothering you?"

J.D. looked at Daniel, and their eyes met. He was her best friend.

Was, she reminded herself. *Before I knew who I really was and where I really belonged.*

"Yes."

She couldn't stop thinking about him.

After dinner, the girls went back to the dormitory. J.D. stayed away from the group, sitting on her bed and trying to think. She ignored their laughter, tuned out their games. It was like nothing out of the ordinary had happened that day. It was like Ilana had never existed.

J.D. wondered how it would feel to be unstable, on the verge of a circuit overload.

Her head felt fuzzy, her body jittery, her chest tight.

Would it feel like that?

Without a word to the other girls, she walked out of the dormitory and headed for the bathroom. She just needed some water. She needed some space.

But once at the sink, her hand on the cup dispenser, she started to shake. *Ilana needed water, too,* she thought. *But she never got it.*

The door swung open, and J.D. quickly brushed her eyes dry. No one could know that her insides were still churning. That seemed important, though she didn't know why.

"You're talking to me whether you like it or not," a boy's voice said.

She whirled around. Daniel was standing in front of the door. "I rigged the lock," he said. "No one's coming in until we talk — and no one's going out."

J.D. crossed her arms. A lock couldn't stop her, or any of the other girls, but it seemed Daniel didn't know that. "You're not supposed to be in here."

"Oh, you're allowed to ambush me in the guys'

bathroom, but I can't come in here?" he asked, smirking.

She had cornered him in the boys' bathroom at the Center, just after they'd first met. She had forced him to talk to her. But this was different.

"That was a long time ago," she said.

"That was a few *weeks* ago."

"A lot has changed," she insisted.

"Yeah. *You*."

"It's not good for me to talk to you," she said. "It's disruptive. I need to move on from my past. This is my home now, and I'm happy here."

"What are you talking about?" he said. "What did they do to you?"

"They did nothing to me," she said. "This is who I am. This is where I belong."

He strode across the room and grabbed her shoulders, shaking her. "This is *not* who you are."

She knocked his arms away. "You don't know who I am — and you don't know what I can do."

"I know you've turned into some kind of zombie," he said. "I see you walking around here with Sykes like he's your best buddy. Did you forget what he did to you?"

"That was all a misunderstanding."

"And what about . . . Look, I don't know if you've seen her yet, but I'm sure it was her. I passed right by her. I was afraid she saw me, but I guess she didn't. It's your — the woman who you thought was —"

"Dr. Mersenne," J.D. said coolly. "I know she's alive. She works here."

"And that doesn't *bother* you?" he asked incredulously. "What, you actually like it here?"

"I am happy here. Where else should I be?" she snapped, anger flaring. "Back in the police station where you left me?"

"So that's what this is about? I told you —"

"You betrayed me!"

"I was trying to help you!"

"I know!" she retorted, trying not to shout. As the words came out, she realized it was true. "I know," she said again, quieter. "And I'm not mad anymore. Really. It all worked out, because I found my way here."

"LysenCorp headquarters," Daniel said. "Ground zero for your evil overlords."

J.D. shook her head. "We were wrong about that. I know what we thought, but . . . it's complicated."

"No. Something's wrong," he said. "Something's different about you."

"What's different is that I'm happy." And even though it wasn't quite true, she wanted it to be. "But . . ." She touched his arm lightly, then jerked her hand away, crossing her arms again. "I'm glad you're here. Even though you shouldn't be. I missed you. I just don't get . . . how are you here?"

"That work release program at the Center," he explained. "Some rep from LysenCorp showed up and said he could take a few of us, room and board for custodial work. And I knew this was my chance — to rescue you."

"Except —"

"Yeah." He looked down. "Except you don't want to be rescued. Got it."

"I'm sorry, I just . . ."

She glanced at the door, wondering how long it would be before someone tried to come in. "I shouldn't be talking to you," she said. "It's against the rules."

He grinned. "Since when do you care about rules?"

"It's very important to follow the rules," she said.

"Stop talking like that! It's creeping me out."

"Like what?" she asked, offended. "I'm talking like myself."

"No, you're talking like some zombie they've got programmed. 'It's very important to follow the rules,'" he said in an emotionless monotone. "That's not you!"

J.D. leaned back against the sinks. "You don't know everything about me."

"So tell me," he urged her. "Tell me everything."

And so she did, starting with the day she'd arrived at the Institute and realized that everything she thought she knew was wrong. She told him about the other girls and her classes, about how much she still hated Dr. Mersenne, and about how her telekinesis was real and finally under her control. And she told him about Ilana.

"So they're keeping you prisoner here, drugging you into submission, training you for who knows what, and they've got you convinced it's all for your own good?"

"Were you even listening?" she asked angrily. "It *is* for our own good. We're dangerous. In the outside world . . ." She shook her head. "I need to be here. They're teaching me how to control myself."

"*They're* controlling you," Daniel argued. "And the J.D. I know wouldn't go for that."

He didn't understand. He couldn't, she realized, because he wasn't like her. He was normal. "You should go," she said, trying not to show her anger or her disappointment. "You shouldn't be here."

"Fine." He walked to the door. "But I'll be watching. And next time you pass me in the hallway, maybe you can at least —"

"Wait."

Daniel stopped with his hand on the doorknob. "What?"

"What you said before, about how I was ignoring you in the halls? You really saw me?"

"What do you mean? Of course I did — and you saw me. Every day. We walked right past each other."

She bit down on her lower lip, not wanting to believe him. But it was Daniel, and he wouldn't lie. "I didn't see you," she admitted. "I don't remember that ever happening."

"Yesterday afternoon?" he prompted her. "Right after lunch? You were walking with Sykes."

"Where?" she asked. "On the way to the greenhouse?"

"No, in the same place as always — over in the east wing, going into that room with the red door. What greenhouse?"

The red door? She'd never seen a room with a red door in the Institute. At least not when she was awake.

"You must be wrong," she told Daniel, trying not to think about her dream. "After lunch yesterday I was in the greenhouse with Dr. Sykes. Like always."

Daniel gave her a strange look. "J.D., I know what I saw."

"I was in the greenhouse with Dr. Sykes," she repeated, trying to convince herself. "Same as always. We sat at our table and —"

"Table?" Daniel shook his head. "J.D., I've cleaned the 'greenhouse.' It may say greenhouse on the door, but inside, it's basically a trash dump. It's where they store the toxic stuff before it gets disposed of every week."

"You must be talking about some other room," J.D. said, confused.

"The greenhouse in the north wing, just down the hall from the cafeteria, right?"

J.D. nodded.

"Then we're talking about the same place. I don't

know what you do with Sykes every afternoon, but you're not having some tea party in a room that doesn't exist."

A strangely familiar emotion washed over her. It took her a minute to place it: terror.

"You have to go," J.D. said quickly. "Before someone finds you here, you have to go."

"Not unless you agree to meet me again. Something's going on here, J.D. And we've got to figure it out. Together, remember?"

"Fine. Tomorrow," she said. "Can you sneak out in the middle of the night?"

"You know me. I can sneak out of anywhere, anytime."

"Tomorrow night," she said. "Two A.M., right here."

"You'll be here?" he asked, narrowing his eyes. "You won't back out because it's against the rules?"

"I'll be here," she said, giving him a real smile for the first time. "I promise."

Something was very wrong.

She didn't want to believe Daniel; she didn't want to lose the only real home she'd ever known.

But for the first time, there were questions. Too many questions.

When the tray of medication came around that night, she put the yellow pill in her mouth and she gulped down the water. But she didn't swallow. Instead she got into bed with the bitter pill tucked under her tongue.

She heard Dr. Sykes's voice in her mind: *What happened to Ilana could happen to you.*

But Daniel was there, too. *They've got you drugged into submission.*

Dr. A. knew who she was. He understood her, and he understood how to protect her. She had done horrible things, unspeakable, *unthinkable* things. Dr. Sykes knew it all, and didn't reject her — and he was the only one who could teach her how to repair herself and stop her from killing again. But he had also lied to her.

Daniel had always told her the truth.

He was my best friend, she thought. *Maybe he still is.*

She spit out the pill.

control

That night, she dreamed again of the red door. And in the morning, she palmed her medication, slipping it under her mattress when no one was looking. She kept a smile fixed on her face but couldn't imagine that anyone would believe it. How could they?

Everything was the same as it had always been. The white walls were the same, the classes were the same, the routine was the same, the girls were the same. Silent, unquestioning, happy. Floating.

All except J.D., who felt like she was seeing everything for the first time. She was seeing the Institute the way Daniel saw it. And she had questions. Many questions.

But she knew better than to ask.

After lunch, the other girls filed off down a

corridor for their advanced class. J.D. started down the hall in the opposite direction, toward Sykes's office. They were due for another meeting in the greenhouse.

The greenhouse that, according to Daniel, didn't exist.

It was the same as every other day, except this day, J.D. was awake. If something was going on that she didn't know about, today was the day she would find out. She just hoped that Dr. A. didn't find out she hadn't taken her medication. He always seemed to know what she was going to do before she did it. *Not this time,* she told herself.

A guard stopped her midway down the hall.

"Not today," he said. "Go back to the dormitory. Someone will come for you."

He knows, J.D. thought in alarm. Dr. A. had somehow found out that she had disobeyed, and now she was going to be punished.

She smiled and nodded, knowing it was best to show no fear. She obeyed. And back in the dormitory, she waited, sitting on the edge of her bed, a nervous flutter in her stomach.

Dr. Mersenne arrived a few minutes later.

Behave, J.D. thought. *You're supposed to be happy.*

You're supposed to be floating. She twisted her lips into something that looked like a smile. "Hi, Dr. Mersenne."

"Get up," the doctor snapped.

"Where's Dr. A.?"

"Too busy to waste his time with you."

"And you're not?" J.D. retorted. She couldn't help it. Dr. Mersenne's obvious hatred only fueled her own. And the anger helped keep her head clear, so she embraced it.

"I'm busier than you know," Dr. Mersenne said. "But I've got my orders. And so do you. Get up."

J.D. knew she should get up. But she stayed seated. Just to prove that she could. It felt good to disobey. It felt new.

"Just drop the rebellious act and follow me, because we both know you will eventually, and I don't have time for games."

"What if I don't?"

Dr. Mersenne shrugged. "Then I'll just have to make you."

"You can't make me do anything!" J.D. shouted, leaping off the bed. She knew it wasn't smart, especially not after what had happened yesterday, but she couldn't stop herself.

Dr. Mersenne sighed. "I suppose it's time we see about that." She unclipped a familiar gray device from her belt, and J.D. gasped in horror. She lunged toward the doctor, but not quickly enough. A button was pressed.

J.D. waited for the pain.

Instead, there was music.

The melody was sweet and haunting. Sad. Familiar. As it played inside her head, she felt her will drift away. And that, too, was familiar.

She drifted along with it, rising out of her body, which felt very far away. It felt like it belonged to someone else.

Hold on, she thought, trying to break free from the music, trying to speak, trying to move. But she was frozen in place, her mind locked away from her body, and the music played on.

It had happened before, the strange melody and the feeling of powerlessness, like her mind was trapped behind foggy glass, forced to watch a body that was no longer her own. That was before she'd come home to the Institute, and each time, she'd been able to yank herself out of stasis. She'd been able to bring herself back just in time.

But this time, there was no return. There was nothing to fight.

Her lips stayed closed, her voice silent. And as the music swelled, it was all she could do to keep from floating away completely. It would have been so easy to let her body slip away, to fade from the world that she was no longer a part of, to disappear. She held on. She stayed awake, she watched.

But she still had to obey.

"More progress than I'd thought," Dr. Mersenne murmured. Then, louder, "Follow me."

J.D.'s body took one step forward, then another. Her legs moved awkwardly at first, the stiff and jerking motions of a marionette. But gradually the gait smoothed, and her arms swung at her sides as she followed Dr. Mersenne down one white corridor, then another, until they reached the red door marked ENCODING.

The music played.

And in her mind, silently, helplessly, J.D. screamed.

The first room was small and dark, and J.D. saw the chair. It was metal, with a high back and leather straps, just like in her dream.

"That's behind you now," Dr. Mersenne said. "Today you graduate. Follow me." She crossed the room, walking through a door on the other side. Helpless to do anything but what she'd been ordered, J.D. followed.

The room was large and light and dominated by a long conference table. Ansel Sykes sat at the head of it. He was surrounded by men in black suits, men J.D. didn't recognize.

"Stop," Dr. Mersenne said.

She stopped. The music in her head played on.

Dr. Sykes smiled. "I see you've started without us, Serena."

"It was necessary," Dr. Mersenne said. "We didn't want a scene. And I must admit, the reimplantation seems to have gone even better than you'd expected."

"No problems?" Sykes asked, getting up from the table.

Dr. Mersenne shook her head. "Establishment of control was instantaneous and absolute."

J.D. stood frozen as Ansel Sykes circled her slowly. "Excellent. Aren't you proud of how far you've come, J.D.?"

J.D. didn't speak. Her eyes faced forward, staring blankly at the wall.

What are you doing to me? she screamed in her head.

Dr. Sykes laughed. "Well, no need to answer now, of course. Not while you're . . . indisposed." He turned to the men seated at the table. "As you can see, she will respond only to the person operating her controller. An excellent safeguard to ensure the correct orders are followed."

"J.D., go sit in the corner and wait," Dr. Mersenne said. "And smile."

There was a chair in the corner. J.D. sat. She waited. And she could feel her lips frozen in a smile.

Somewhere inside of her, she had the power to stop them, she thought. She had the power to destroy them all. But she couldn't access it. She couldn't move a finger. She couldn't stop smiling.

Ansel Sykes retook his place at the head of the table, and Dr. Mersenne sat down to his right. "Gentlemen," he began, "as you've seen in your reports, upon her arrival at the Institute the subject's system was flooded with Lyseptican. In the past, we have administered the treatment in small doses, allowing it to build up in the system over several years, accompanied by a program of subliminal commands. But time constraints demanded a different tactic. And thanks to your generous financial support, I was able to design an alternate approach. Obviously, there were risks inherent in administering so much Lyseptican at once in the manner we did, but the protocol was a success. With the addition of daily follow-up treatments, the subject's Lyseptican intake has reached the levels she was at before her unfortunate disappearance. As you can see, the reimplantation of subconscious commands has been complete. With intensive encoding sessions and twice-daily administration of a mild tranquilizer, subject is fully back under our control. I propose we —"

"I'd like to see some further evidence that she really is under control," one of the suited men said. "We wouldn't want a repeat of . . . past events."

"Response to the light protocol was promising even before the treatment and has now been rendered absolute," Dr. Sykes said. "And we learned yesterday that disciplinary safeguards have also been reimplanted to our satisfaction. All that remains is ensuring that she responds adequately to the auditory cues and is able to take orders."

"Exactly," the same man said. "It's the receptivity to orders that I'd like to confirm."

Dr. Sykes pulled his own gray device out of his pocket. "Dr. Mersenne, we'll transfer the control to me now." Dr. Mersenne nodded, and they each pressed a button on their devices. "Stand up, J.D.," he ordered. "And show us all that beautiful smile."

She stood.

His voice sounded both very far away and inside her head at the same time. It twisted and twined itself with the music, demanding submission. She hated him.

She smiled.

Dr. Sykes pointed at the man who had spoken up. "Lift Mr. Hennessy and his chair five feet in the air, J.D. Slowly and carefully, please."

She felt it stirring within her, a stroke of electricity jolting through her, as the warm heat rippled across her body. There was a surge of energy, and she wanted Sykes to pay, wanted to erase his smirk, to silence the music.

But Mr. Hennessy and his chair rose five feet off the ground. Slowly and carefully. As requested.

"Put me down!" the man shouted.

"Put him down now, J.D.," Ansel Sykes sputtered through his laughter.

And she complied.

That was the beginning. They ran her through a series of tasks, some easy, some difficult. And she did what they said, without fail, without control.

She had given up on the silent screaming. There was no point in fighting.

"She's ready," Sykes said firmly.

J.D. sat in the corner, waiting for orders.

"She's been fully encoded with her mission parameters," he continued. "I suggest she now rejoin the other subjects. The deadline is only a few days away, and it's imperative that she be fully reimmersed in the program."

"With all due respect to Ansel," Dr. Mersenne said, "I think it would be unwise to proceed at this point."

"We have no choice," Dr. Sykes snapped.

"A number of the other subjects have shown potential and might be able to replace —"

"Unwise and unnecessary to make a change at

this point," Dr. Sykes said. "Especially after we went to all the trouble of getting her back. She's ready. And let's not forget that number thirteen is unlike any of the other subjects. We'd be fools not to take advantage of her unique abilities."

"I would like to hear why Dr. Mersenne feels so strongly that this is ill-advised," one of the men in suits said. Dr. Sykes frowned.

"The subject is unpredictable," Dr. Mersenne insisted. "We still have no idea what caused the memory loss after the explosion, or why it eroded most of our implanted commands as well. It's *possible* that Ansel's ill-advised procedure has solved the problem and regained control —"

"I assure you that I —"

"But it's *also* possible," she spoke over him, "that this is just a temporary fix. That even with all the Lyseptican in the world, her brain will still prove resistant to programming. For obvious reasons, this subject's brain has always reacted differently from those of the other subjects. She has always been stronger, always required a higher dosage to prime her for encoding. It's my concern that now, after all that's happened, she may actually have developed the ability to resist."

Mr. Hennessy leaned forward, placing his elbows on the conference table. "So your official recommendation, Dr. Mersenne?"

"We dispose of the subject and replace her with one of the others. I would suggest number one, who goes by the name Mara. She's coming along nicely."

"Dr. Sykes, your response?"

"Dr. Mersenne's fears are groundless," he replied. "And with only six days before deployment, second-guessing ourselves could prove disastrous. It's my enthusiastic recommendation that we notify the client we are going forward *exactly* as planned."

J.D. stood motionless in the hallway, staring at the red door.

"Congratulations, Ansel," Dr. Mersenne said. "You got your way yet again."

"It is my program," Dr. Sykes said. "What did you expect?"

Dr. Mersenne shook her head. "She can resist if she wants to. You know that. She has the power to fight."

I have the power to fight, J.D. thought, and with a surge of strength and hope, she struggled to regain control. It was like trying to smash through a brick wall with her fists.

Useless.

"If she realized there was a battle, perhaps." Ansel Sykes chuckled. "But she has no idea. And as long as that remains the case, we have nothing to worry about."

"Then I suggest you not antagonize her," Dr. Mersenne said, "or the results could be ugly."

Sykes raised an eyebrow. "Antagonize her? Haven't you noticed? The subject adores me. I'm her beloved Dr. A." He laughed again, breaking off as his body was racked by a coughing fit. Finally, he caught his breath. "It's *you* she hates, Serena. She believes I'm the only one she can trust." He shook his head. "And she thinks she's so smart."

"You underestimate her," Dr. Mersenne warned.

"You underestimate *me*." Sykes nodded to a guard positioned in the hallway. "Dr. Mersenne here is a little *afraid* of our prize subject. Please accompany them back to the dormitory."

"Ansel, that's not necessary —"

"It is if I say it is," Dr. Sykes said, and before she could answer, he walked away.

"Come, J.D." Dr. Mersenne barked.

And like a dog, she did.

Dr. Mersenne ordered her into the empty dormitory, then into bed. She tucked in J.D.'s motionless body while the guard waited by the door.

You did this before, J.D. thought, staring at the ceiling because she'd been ordered to lie on her back. *You tucked me in. When you were my mother.*

Then, the woman had bent down and kissed her forehead. As she leaned over the bed, J.D. almost expected her to do it again now, but she only tapped her fingers against the small gray device clipped to her belt.

"He doesn't see what's going on here," she murmured, so softly J.D. almost couldn't make out the words. "But I do. I know you're dangerous — if you want to be."

Dr. Mersenne glanced at the guard, then rested a hand lightly on J.D.'s forehead. Her touch burned. J.D.'s eyes still stared blankly ahead.

"You were feeling sick after lunch," Dr. Mersenne said. "You came back to your room to take a nap. You went straight to sleep. You never saw me, you never saw Dr. Sykes. You just slept. Close your eyes now."

J.D.'s eyes closed.

"When I tell you to sleep, you'll sleep, and when you wake up, you'll remember nothing that happened after lunch today."

I will remember, J.D. thought. *I'll remember that you're my enemy and that this place is a prison. I'll remember everything.*

"Sleep now," Dr. Mersenne said, her hand still resting on J.D.'s forehead.

You have the power to fight, J.D. reminded herself. *Fight.*

"Sleep," Dr. Mersenne murmured.

She struggled against the dark fog filling her mind; she tried to force her eyes open. But the music, which had never stopped, swelled and crested and echoed in her head, driving her thoughts away. Her eyes never fluttered, her lungs expanded and contracted in a smooth, even rhythm, and her clouded mind lost its grip.

Remember.

Fight.

"Sleep," Dr. Mersenne ordered.

She slept.

lies

J.D. recoiled at his touch without knowing why.

"It's just me," he said, brushing her hair off her
forehead. "Dr. A."

She bolted upright. Ansel Sykes was sitting on the
edge of the bed. "What's happening? What am I
doing here?"

And what are you *doing here?* she thought in alarm.

"You got sick," he said softly. "After lunch. Don't
you remember?"

Once he said it, she did remember.

"I was feeling sick after lunch," she said. "I came
back to my room to take a nap. I went straight to
sleep."

"I was quite worried when I heard," he said. "But
you're looking okay now. How do you feel?"

"I feel . . ." She felt like she was missing something,

like there was something she was supposed to do. It played at the edges of her mind, skittering away whenever she got close. "Fine." But it wasn't fine. When Dr. Sykes smiled at her, everything felt wrong. She jerked away at his touch.

It felt like there was something gone, something she had forgotten. And when it came to that, J.D. trusted her instincts. She was an expert on forgetting.

She pushed herself to remember.

I was feeling sick after lunch, she thought. *I came back to my room to take a nap. I went straight to sleep.* There was nothing else.

"J.D.? Is something wrong?"

Another instinct kicked in: *Lie.*

She shook her head and smiled. "Everything's fine, Dr. A. Why wouldn't it be?"

He patted the blanket and stood up. "Well, I should let you get some rest before dinner. I just wanted to come by to see how you were feeling — and to deliver the good news in person."

"What is it?" she asked, trying to sound excited. *I could attack him right now,* she thought — and then remembered the device in his pocket. She remembered the pain. She behaved.

It felt like she was at war with herself, and the

struggle was tearing her apart. There was what she knew to be true — and then, even without evidence or logic, there was what she believed. And she believed she was in danger.

"As usual, your remarkable progress astounds me," Dr. Sykes said. "You're doing better than any of us could have hoped. So I'm pleased to say that, as of tomorrow, you'll be joining the rest of the girls in their advanced lessons."

J.D. shivered. She should have been happy and proud, but all she felt was dread.

"Something wrong?" Dr. Sykes asked again.

"No," she said quickly, snuggling deeper into the blanket. "I'm just cold. Maybe I'm still a little sick."

This means no more meetings in the "greenhouse," she thought. *Or whatever happens — wherever he takes me.* It should have been a good thing. So why did she feel so uneasy?

"I should let you sleep more," he said. "You can join your friends for dinner tonight, but only if you're feeling up to it. And if you start feeling worse, you'll let someone know immediately. Promise?"

J.D. nodded. "Promise."

"Then rest up. You've got a big day tomorrow,"

he said, turning off the lights on the way out of the room. "Oh, and J.D.?"

His voice wafted through the darkness, and she imagined she could almost feel its slimy trail crawling across her skin.

"What?" she asked.

"You've made me very proud."

"I was feeling sick after lunch," she told Daniel. "I came back to my room to take a nap. I went straight to sleep. That's it."

As planned, they were meeting up in the girls' bathroom long after everyone else had gone to sleep.

"Sick how?" Daniel asked.

"What do you mean? I don't know. Sick."

"Well, sick like you ate something bad? Or sick like a headache? A runny nose? Dizziness? Sick how?"

Sick like Ilana? she wondered. Dr. Sykes had warned her how important it was to take her pills, and instead, she continued to spit them out as soon as she got a chance. Was she freeing herself from his control, like Daniel suspected? Or was she turning her back on the only thing that could keep her brain from destroying itself?

"I don't know," she snapped. "Just sick."

Daniel leaned back against the tile wall. "How can you not know? Think."

She remembered being at lunch. *That* she remembered vividly. She'd sat with Mara on her left and an empty chair on her right — Ilana's chair. There had been hot dogs and overcooked French fries. Katherine had spilled a glass of water and J.D. had helped mop it up with a thick sheaf of napkins. Her hot dog bun had been stale, but the ketchup made it soggy. They ate in silence.

After lunch, the rest of the girls had filed down the hall in one direction, and J.D. had started off in the other. As always. And then —

I was feeling sick. I came back to my room to take a nap. I went straight to sleep.

"I don't know," she said. "I don't remember."

"Picture yourself at lunch," Daniel suggested. "Did you have a headache? Did you get dizzy while you were walking down the hall? Did you —"

"I don't know!" J.D. shouted, forgetting to keep her voice down. "I was at lunch, and then I felt sick. I came back to my room to take a nap. I went to sleep."

"You *said* that," Daniel said. "*Exactly* that. What else?"

"Nothing!" There was a stabbing pain behind her eyes. She winced and grabbed her head.

"What?"

She closed her eyes for a moment and pressed her palms against her eyelids. The pain faded away. *Why can't I remember?* she thought in frustration, and the pain came back.

"Headache," she whispered.

"You remember having a headache?"

"No. Now. Headache." Her head was pulsing; it felt like her brain was expanding against her skull.

I felt sick. I went to my room to take a nap. I went to sleep. That's it.

I believe it.

The pain faded to a dull ache. And then, a moment later, it drifted away.

"J.D., what is it, what's wrong?" Daniel asked in alarm.

"It's fine," she assured him, drawing in a deep breath. "I'm fine. I just . . . let's not talk about this afternoon anymore, okay?"

"If you don't want to —"

"I just can't." Something about the words were familiar — and suddenly, she gasped.

"What?"

"Ilana — my friend here, she . . ." J.D. chewed the edge of her thumbnail, trying to make sense of what she'd just remembered. "Something went wrong with her yesterday. With her . . . brain. But before that, I was asking her about what she did in the afternoon, in these advanced lessons that I wasn't allowed to go to, and she wouldn't tell me. She just kept saying the same thing, over and over again. They learned stuff. I wanted to know more, and I thought she didn't want to tell me. But she said she *couldn't* tell me. And she got this really bad headache all of a sudden — she got a lot of headaches, and then . . ." J.D.'s voice trailed off as she remembered the fight. It was the last conversation she'd had with Ilana, maybe the last conversation they would ever have.

"I have to figure out what they're doing to us here. It's something horrible. I don't know what, but — why are you smiling?"

Daniel's face was lit up with a wide grin. "Because you're back. You're *you* again."

J.D. wanted to argue that she'd never left, but she knew he was right.

"I have to figure out what's going on," she said. "I have to stop whatever they're doing to me."

"*We* have to stop it," Daniel said. "Together, right?"

At that, J.D.'s smile was almost as wide as his. She nodded. "Together."

"So when do we go?" Daniel asked.

"What? Go where?"

Daniel looked at her like she hadn't been paying attention. "We have to get you out of here. And soon, before —"

"I'm not leaving," J.D. said firmly.

"Are you kidding me?"

"I can't. Not yet."

Daniel nodded. "You're right, security's tough. But there's a back exit behind the kitchen, and a supply truck shows up around dawn. We could sneak on board while they're unloading and —"

"No. Daniel, I mean, I *can't*." J.D. took a deep breath. It was tempting to think that it would be that easy, that she could just slip out a back entrance and disappear into the world. She could leave the Institute behind and forget all about Dr. Mersenne and Dr. Sykes and whatever they'd done to her.

But she couldn't. And not just because Dr. Sykes would come after her. Although he would.

"I came here for a reason, and I'm not just running away. Not yet. Not until I get the truth." She paused. "You're smiling again."

"Can't help it."

"Well, stop it. This is serious. Things are bad, and they're probably going to get worse."

"Then why are *you* smiling?"

She couldn't help it, either. "Because it feels kind of good to . . ."

"What?"

"To be me again," she admitted. *To fight.* And at that thought, her smile faded. "But what if . . . ?"

"What?" Daniel asked quietly.

"How am I supposed to fight, when I don't even know what I'm fighting?"

"You can fight anything, J.D.," he said. "You're strong. You have to know you can fight."

Something about his words sounded familiar — and true.

I am strong, she reminded herself. *I can fight. I've done it before.*

But something told her that whatever she'd faced in the past was nothing compared to what was coming next. She would *have* to be strong, because this was going to be the fight of her life.

mission

J.D. barely slept. And when she finally managed to fall asleep, there were the dreams. She woke up covered in sweat, shivering. But the nightmares only left a residue of fear. J.D. couldn't remember what they had been about. She just knew she was afraid.

Eyes red and drooping, she forced herself to make it through the morning's classes. Her concentration waned with every hour, and the more tired she got, the more difficult it was to keep smiling.

Lunch that day was a mushy, flavorless meat loaf that reminded her of the food at the Center. From the way Daniel winked when he plopped it onto her plate, she suspected he was thinking the same thing. She watched him all through the meal, hoping no one would notice her staring. It was comforting to know he was there.

But then lunch ended, and the girls filed out of the room and down the hall. *I'm on my own now,* J.D. thought as she followed them. She should have been afraid, but she couldn't help feeling a flutter of excitement. She was about to discover what happened at the "advanced lessons" — and maybe it would get her one step closer to finding her answers. Or at least help her figure out the right questions to ask.

She walked quietly down the hall, single file after the other girls. They kept their eyes on the floor, but J.D. looked up, memorizing their path and searching for doors that might lead to the outside.

The guard at the head of the line pulled out his gray device.

The music began.

J.D. pressed her hands against her ears, but it didn't help. The melody was coming from inside her head, and it was getting louder. "No," she whispered, unable to force out a sound. *Fight.*

But the music swelled, and her arms dropped to her sides, and her mind drifted.

"Follow me," called the guard at the head of the line.

The girls walked forward in lockstep, their arms swinging rhythmically back and forth, marking the same beat. J.D. tried to stop walking or stomp her feet, but she couldn't even slow herself down. She couldn't even blink.

Her body was a machine, and it was under someone else's control.

No fear, she thought, as the girls trooped down the hall. Her legs walked, her arms swung, her lungs breathed, and none of it belonged to her anymore.

Let go, the music warbled to her. *Give in.*

It would have been so easy. There was no point in resisting; it accomplished nothing. Only sapped her energy. Maybe she should just accept that she was locked up inside herself. She could curl up inside her mind, release her worries, and wait for it all to end. There was no reason to hold on. But she did it anyway.

The green liquid burned.

There was a silver needle embedded in her left arm, and attached to it, a thin plastic tube stretching to an IV. The liquid seeped into her veins. It felt like a stream of tiny knives.

Her wrists were strapped to the chair. Her left arm lay palm up, to expose the vein.

In her head, the music played on.

She stared straight ahead, but out of the corner of her eyes she could see girls to her left and right. Each had her own chair; each had her own IV. Each was silent.

"The Lyseptican primes the brain," Dr. Sykes said as he wandered up and down the row of girls. A man in a dark blue suit followed closely behind him. "Under normal hypnosis, a subject will never do anything he or she wouldn't do while conscious. But with the addition of the Lyseptican, we are able to embed commands far more deeply — and there is no limit on what those commands may be."

"And you assure me that your hypnotic trigger will work remotely?" the man asked with a thick accent.

"Each subject has an implant that plays the music directly into her auditory complex. Depending on the melody, subjects will either obey orders or carry out a set of preprogrammed tasks," Dr. Sykes said. "This is all explained in my reports. Is it really necessary to go over it again? You know better than anyone that time is of the essence."

"I am sure your benefactors at LysenCorp have explained my position, Doctor," the man said. "I have a significant amount of money invested in this operation, and you will do anything I deem necessary to give me full assurance that nothing will go awry."

"I've given you no cause to doubt. You've seen demonstrations of what we can —"

The man's voice was quiet but dangerous. "You seem to forget the most recent field test, Doctor. You lost control of your prize subject."

"A minor setback. We've since corrected the problem." The men paused in front of J.D. She continued to stare blankly ahead. *Don't panic,* she told herself. *Pay attention.* She wouldn't be a prisoner forever, and maybe she would hear something that would help set her free. "As you can see, number thirteen has been brought back fully into the protocol."

"You know she's crucial to the mission."

What mission? J.D. thought in alarm. *What are they brainwashing me to do?*

"And I assure you," Dr. Sykes said, "she will be ready."

"And what about the other one, number six?"

"That was an anticipated casualty," Dr. Sykes said. "In addition to mild sedatives, the subjects receive periodic medication to boost their telekinetic abilities, and in a *very* few number of cases, the medication has proven to be . . . damaging. Number six has been replaced. The other subjects are all strong, you can be sure of that."

"You don't imagine this medication could also have caused the problems with number thirteen?"

"She doesn't receive it," Dr. Sykes replied. "Her abilities do not need enhancements. They have bloomed of their own accord, due to her own . . . special circumstances. She's our strongest subject and the one *least* likely to bow under pressure. I guarantee it. This is why she's been assigned the key role."

"Strength is one thing, Doctor. But I'm looking for control. I need to know that these girls will carry out their mission."

"You have my personal guarantee on that. Our control is absolute."

"I should hope so, Doctor. I trust I don't need to warn you of the consequences of failure. Very serious consequences. So please, walk me through the procedure. Convince me that I'm getting my money's worth."

Sykes sighed. "If you insist."

A man in white arrived at J.D.'s chair and fumbled with something over her head. A cold metal mask was attached to her face, and she gazed into the dark.

"Each subject receives a daily reinforcement of objectives. And our technology enables us to prime each of them with a distinct set of instructions specific to each mission," Sykes's voice said.

Then something hard pressed down on each ear, squeezing her head together, and she heard no more.

She was lost in the darkness and silence, unable to move.

And then the screen lit up.

She saw a crowded city street, filled with people and cars. She heard feet shuffling and scuffling across the pavement, whirring engines, honking horns. And then she felt a chilly wind on her face.

She smelled the car fumes and the rotting bags of garbage lining the street. She was standing on a street corner, watching the traffic speed by.

This isn't real, she thought desperately. But there was no other reality, only this, the street, the people, the cars.

The car.

The long black car. It glowed, as the rest of the world faded to a sepia brown.

He is inside the car, a deep voice warned her. It was Sykes's voice, but it felt like it was coming from inside of her. *Wait for your moment.*

She was on the street, but at the same time she was *watching* herself on the street, still out of control, unable to do anything but stand and watch and wait.

The car came closer, and a black tinted window rolled down. It framed a man's face, and the face glowed bright like the car.

Destroy him, the voice said. *Destroy.*

No! she screamed silently, but she raised her arms, and as the energy shot through her, the car launched off the street, toward the sidewalk, toward the gas station, toward the pumps.

Nooooo! Inside, a scream became a moan became a howl as the car crashed into the pumps and she knew what came next because somehow she had seen it before.

You're strong. It was Daniel's voice; it was a reminder. *You have to know you can fight.* But she couldn't. She didn't know how. And the nightmare continued.

Next came the explosion. The fire. She could still see the man's face as the ball of fire —

"*No!*"

The image froze. And suddenly, it was an image again. She was back in the chair, and instead of the wind, she could feel the metal against her back, the mask bearing down on her face, the green liquid burning through her veins.

And though she was still trapped in silence, she could feel her lips move. "No!" she tried again. It wasn't her imagination. She had spoken.

I can *fight,* she thought, and with a surge of strength, she forced her mind back into her body — and her left thumb twitched. Just once, just for a moment, but she felt it, and it gave her more strength. Enough to move all her fingers, to grip the edge of the chair. The more control she got, the easier it was — and though the music still echoed through her head, it was softer, less insistent, and the numbness began to fade away. She was still strapped down, but straps couldn't stop her, not with her abilities. If she could just gain enough strength to —

A hand slapped down on top of hers. The frozen image on the monitor disappeared, and she was left in darkness again. But she could feel the presence of someone standing in front of her — and, more amazing, she could feel her hand straining against its restraints.

She was strong enough to speak and move, but she wasn't strong enough to escape the iron grip that locked her arm against the chair. And she wasn't strong enough to squirm out of the way as another needle punctured her skin.

I did it, she thought as her strength ebbed and her mind grew foggy. Whatever they'd given her, it worked fast, and it worked well. Her thoughts were slow and muffled, and a current dragged her down beneath a dark surface. *I fought back,* she told herself as she drifted down into the black.

And I can do it again.

"Well, what do you think? J.D.? Hello?"

J.D. blinked and shook her head, trying to clear it. "What?"

Mara rolled her eyes. "She *said,* what do you think they'll serve for dinner tonight?"

What happened? J.D. thought, looking around in confusion. She was in the dormitory, sitting in a small circle with some of the other girls. But . . . how did they get there? They'd been at lunch, and then afterward, they'd walked down the hall single file, and . . .

"If it's meat loaf again, I may throw up," a girl named Leslie complained.

"How did we . . . ?" J.D. pressed her hand against the wall, trying to assure herself it was real. "What's going on? How are we back here?"

Leslie looked at her like she was crazy. "What are you talking about? We had our advanced lesson, and then we came back here before dinner. Like every day. Are you okay?"

"She's fine," Mara said. "She's just looking for attention. Probably hopes that we'll run to Dr. A. and she'll get some more special treatment."

"No, I just . . ." J.D. shook her head again, harder this time. *Advanced lessons . . . yes.* That's where they'd been headed after lunch. And then . . .

We had class.

We learned many valuable and interesting things.

We came back to the dormitory.

That was exactly how she remembered it. *But what did I learn?* she thought. Daniel would want to know. *What did we do?*

Many valuable and interesting things.

She saw herself sitting in a classroom, listening and obeying. She saw herself coming back to the dorm room. And here she was. It all made sense.

But it all felt wrong.

"Do you guys remember what we did in class this afternoon?"

"Stuff," Leslie said, brushing a hand through her hair.

"But what kind of stuff?"

"You know. Stuff."

"What's your problem?" Mara asked. "You were right there with us. Or is your 'amnesia' back again?" She blew out a sharp burst of air. "You're such a faker."

"I'm not faking anything!"

"Well, then maybe you're falling apart, just like Ilana, and we should —"

"I'm fine," J.D. said quickly. "Just forget it."

"It's not so easy for some of us," Mara sneered. "Some of us actually manage to remember things once in a while."

J.D. didn't answer. *We came back to the dorm,* she thought, and she remembered that it was true. But she couldn't remember their route, or which teacher had led them, or who had been standing behind her in line.

How can I not remember? she thought, her head throbbing with sudden pain. *If it was only a few minutes ago, how can it be gone already? What's happening?*

Something. She knew that much, at least.

And as the dull ache turned into a stabbing pain, she knew she was on the right track.

The green liquid.

The chair.

The black car.

The green liquid.

The ball of fire.

And it burned.

It burned.

J.D. bolted up in bed, closing her eyes against the darkness and listening to her ragged breathing.

We had class. We learned many valuable and interesting things. We came back to the dormitory. But the memories were too thin and too weak, and they shattered under the weight of the dreams. Dimly, she saw herself sitting obediently in class. But there was another memory layered on top, superimposed, a terrifying vision of metal chairs, of leather straps and sharp needles. Of music and death.

They're brainwashing me, she thought, shaking. Sleep fell away, but the dreams, the memories, remained, and she had a flash of how it had felt, trapped in her own mind. Helpless to do anything but watch. *They're programming me to kill.*

She had to find Daniel. She had to escape, to tell someone about what was happening, to find a way to set the other girls free. If only she knew more. If only she had some evidence . . .

And then she remembered the pills. She hid a new one under her mattress each morning and each night. It wasn't much, but it was something. She could go to the cops, she could go to the media, she could *force* them to believe her. And then someone would have to help.

I don't even know where I am, she reminded herself. She'd been brought to the Institute unconscious in a van. Even if she managed to get off the property, she wouldn't know where to go next — or how to find her way back.

But I have to try.

She reached under the mattress. The pills were gone. Instead, her fingers closed around something unexpected. She pulled out a scrap of paper, unable to read it in the dark.

I didn't put this there, she thought, terrified. Someone must have figured out that she wasn't taking her pills. But if they had, why hadn't they said something?

J.D. crept out of bed and tiptoed across the room, then slid open the door and let herself into the hallway. She squinted in the light and smoothed out the scrap of paper. There were only a few words on it, and most of them made no sense.

XJ2St634SSnR
GALTON PROJECT
CCCR DEPLOYMENT
EVE TRIALS
SUBJECT 13G

And then at the bottom, after all the words that held no meaning for her, came one word that did.

SYKES

eve

J.D. was getting impatient. There were
only a few hours left before dawn, and she needed to
do something. She just didn't know what.

"You're sure you have no idea where it came from?
Who put it there?" Daniel asked, staring down at
the scrap of paper. She wished he would just give it
back to her. There was something comforting about
holding it in her hand, running her finger along its
torn edges. Maybe because she was still afraid that,
at any moment, it could disappear as quickly as it
had appeared — that she would wake up in bed to
discover that it had just been a dream.

But this was real.

"What do you think it means?" J.D. asked.

Daniel pulled a paper clip out of his pocket and
began twisting and turning it into a metallic pretzel.
"I don't know about most of it, but this" — he

pointed to the nonsense string of numbers and letters — "I could be wrong, but it looks like a computer password."

"If that's true, you think these other words could be file names?" J.D. asked. "Like clues for what we're supposed to be looking for?"

"Could be," Daniel said hesitantly, "but . . ."

"But what?" J.D. grabbed the paper. "We have to go. It's the password to Sykes's computer, it's got to be. This is our chance, Daniel. We can finally get some answers."

Daniel rubbed the back of his neck, scowling. "But think about what you said. That they could be clues for what we're *supposed* to be looking for."

"Yeah, so?"

"So, clues from where? From *whom*? Who decided what we're *supposed* to be doing? And what makes you think we can trust them?"

"I don't know," J.D. admitted. "But what else can we do?"

"We can ignore it," he said. "After what you told me, what they're doing to you . . . J.D., we could just get out of here. *Tonight*. We can tell someone about what's going on here. Someone else can stop Sykes. It doesn't have to be us."

139

"Maybe it doesn't have to be, but . . ."

"But you want it to be," Daniel guessed, sighing.

"Don't you?" she asked. "After everything he's done — to *both* of us — can you really stop now?" She waved the scrap of paper at him. "Aren't you curious? Yes, maybe it's a trap, but maybe it's not. And even if it is . . ."

"You *want* it to be!" Daniel said in surprise.

"What? No, I don't."

"Yes, you do. I can see it in your eyes. You want a fight."

"I do not, I just —" J.D. stopped, and wrapped a fist around the scrap of paper, covering it with her other hand. "I don't want it to be a trap," she said slowly. "Really, I don't. But if it is, we can deal with that. And maybe it would be worth it, to face Sykes, to show him that I'm not scared anymore. That he doesn't fool me anymore. Maybe I do want to fight — but only because I think we can win." She took a deep breath and blushed, realizing how she must sound — like a general rallying her troops for battle. "But we have to both agree," she said. "I'm not dragging you into my fight."

"You really think this could lead us to some answers?" Daniel asked.

She nodded.

"Then you're right. We can't leave before we see it through."

"Are you sure?" she asked.

"You said it yourself, J.D. This is your home. This is your fight. All this stuff—the Institute, brainwashing, mad scientists, your weird superhero 'powers'—I don't get it. But you do. And if you think this is the right thing to do, then I trust you."

"Really? You're going to trust a zombie?" she asked, only half teasing. How could he trust her after everything that had happened? Sykes and Mersenne had played with her mind like a cheap toy, fooling her into believing that everything she knew was a lie, and every lie they told was the truth. Even now that she'd broken through — broken free — she could barely trust herself.

"You're no zombie," he assured her, "not anymore."

"And never again," she said, trying to convince herself as much as him. "I promise."

Three locked doors stood between the girls' dormitory in the north wing and Sykes's office to the west. The staff were strongly discouraged

141

from circulating through the building after dark, and the locks were in place in case they elected to disobey.

But locked doors were no problem. As they arrived at the first one, Daniel pulled out his lock-picking kit. J.D. hesitated for a moment, then grinned, stepped in front of him, and concentrated.

The door whooshed open.

When they reached the second door, Daniel's lock picks stayed in his pocket. And this time, J.D. didn't even pause.

As they hid in a recessed corner, waiting for a pair of guards to pass by, J.D. realized Daniel was staring at her. "What?" she whispered, turning fully toward him. He flinched.

"What is it?" she asked.

He shook his head and brought a finger to his lips, then pointed at the guards. They were still too close. J.D. held her breath and her questions for another several moments, until they were safely alone.

They rushed down the hall. The night was slipping away, and Sykes's office was only a few steps away.

"What's wrong?" she asked quietly.

"Nothing," he said.

"Then why won't you look at me?"

"I'm looking for guards," Daniel said. "In case you forgot, we're on a dangerous secret mission."

"Fine."

They reached the dark door to Sykes's office and stood staring at it for a long moment.

"Well?" Daniel said finally, still not looking at her.

"Well, what?"

"Aren't you going to open it?"

"Tell me what's wrong," J.D. insisted.

"If we stand out here for much longer, someone's going to —"

"Daniel!" She folded her arms across her chest. "We're not going in until you talk."

He stared down at the floor. "It's just . . . what you did, opening the doors . . . with your *mind*? It's crazy." He shook his head. "I can't believe this is happening. And I can't believe you . . ."

"I told you what I could do." J.D. decided not to remind him that she'd told him again and again, but he hadn't believed her. Now he had no choice.

"I know. But knowing it and . . . seeing it. That's different. The things you can do, it's not . . ."

"Normal?" she said bitterly. "Yeah, I get it. I'm a freak. Thanks for reminding me."

He jerked his head up and finally looked at her.

"*No!* That's not it. I mean . . . yeah, it's not normal. You're not normal. You're . . . it's *incredible.*" He gave her a wry smile. "I wish I could do something like that. Something amazing."

J.D. sighed. "No, you really don't."

Daniel put his hand lightly on her shoulder. "J.D. . . ."

"What?"

There was silence as their eyes locked.

"Nothing," he finally said. "Can you just get us in before we get caught?"

She shrugged, and twisted the doorknob. It opened easily, unlocked as always. Daniel's eyes widened, and J.D. winked. Then she swung the door open wide and swept an arm across the threshold. "After you."

J.D. held her breath as she walked over to the computer. She kept imagining Sykes popping up from behind the desk, that knowing smile on his face.

"*I've been expecting you,*" he would say, as if she could never do anything that would surprise him.

You're wrong about me, she thought. *You've always*

been wrong. And then she forced herself to stop thinking about him. Sykes had delayed and distracted her long enough. Tonight, nothing was getting in the way of her search for answers.

The computer was already on, and when J.D. pressed down a random key, a box popped up, asking for a password. Daniel and J.D. exchanged a glance. Then she pulled out the scrap of paper. "Here goes nothing," she said, and, holding her breath, began to type.

XJ2St634SSnR

She hit ENTER. The computer screen went blank. A wave of disappointment crashed over her. Had they guessed wrong? Did the note mean something else entirely?

Password accepted.

The screen flickered and turned green. They stared at a desktop littered with files, then turned to each other, matching grins stretched across their faces. "We did it!" Daniel whispered.

J.D. waved the scrap of paper. "No, *he* did it. Or she. Whoever left this. I just hope they're on our side."

"Let's find out," Daniel suggested. "Start at the top?"

She nodded, and he opened a search box, typing in the first item on the list.

Galton project

The hard drive whirred, and after a moment a list of files popped up on the screen. J.D. clicked open the top one.

Subject 1

> GCA
> TGC
> TGC
> ACT
> TTG
> GCT

The string of letters stretched on for pages.

"What is it?" J.D. breathed.

Daniel scrolled down the file. He shook his head. "I don't know."

"Wait, stop!" J.D. hissed as the letters gave way to words, words that actually made sense.

Name: Arielle Klesmer
   Born: March 30, Wilson, New Jersey
   Subject Identification: April 1
   Subject Retrieval: April 14
   Reassignment: Subject #1, MARA

J.D. looked up from the screen. "What's it supposed to mean?" She smashed her hand against the desk. "What's the point in breaking into the computer if we can't understand anything it says?"

"Shh!" Daniel urged her. "It's just the first file. We'll find something."

But as they clicked through at random, every file was the same. Subject two, subject three, subject four, all came with the same string of letters and, at the bottom, two names. One J.D. had never heard before, and one that belonged to one of her friends.

They were all there, all identified by number. All except her.

Subject thirteen, she thought, remembering the number scrawled on her daily cup of medication. *I'm number thirteen.*

But there was no number thirteen.

She rubbed the tattoo on the back of her neck. LysenCorp had branded each girl with their logo — it wasn't a surprise that they saw the girls as numbers.

"This is it," Daniel said excitedly as a new document popped up on the screen, titled "Concluding Report." It was addressed to the CEO of LysenCorp, and according to the date, it had been written thirteen years before.

RE: Galton Project

Twelve subjects bearing the genetic marker have been identified and retrieved. Parents in each case believe the subject was a victim of Sudden Infant Death Syndrome. Authorities suspect nothing. Administration of Lyseptican to begin immediately, encoding to follow. Telekinetic abilities expected to appear within sixteen months. Development of medical protocol to boost abilities is proceeding on schedule. It remains likely that treatment will destabilize neural network; when administered in concert with sedation, most subjects should survive.

Note: Eve Trials continue with Subject 13G —
success is imminent.
Ansel Sykes

Daniel gaped at the screen. "It's kidnapping!"

"What?" J.D. knew she should be trying to figure
out what the memo meant, but she couldn't help
staring at the last line. *Eve Trials continue with Subject
13G.* It was about her, it had to be. But what could
it mean?

"They told your parents you were dead — all of
you — and they brought you here!" Daniel said.
"They kidnapped a bunch of babies and loaded them
up with experimental drugs. It's insane! Who *does*
that?" He clicked open an Internet browser, then
slammed his hand against the keyboard. "Fire-
walled!" He leaned across the desk and flicked on the
printer. "If we can't email this out, we've got to print
it, we've got to get evidence, tell someone what's
happening here, send these guys to jail, and — J.D.,
come on, don't you get what this means?"

"We have to find the Eve Trials," J.D. said,
commandeering the keyboard as the printer began
spitting out pages.

"Maybe we should just get out now with what we've got, before someone —"

"*No,*" J.D. said firmly. "We've come this far. I have to know."

But the search function came up empty. There were no documents containing "Eve Trials" or anything like it. "It's got to be here," J.D. muttered, running the search a second time, and then a third. "If there's no file . . ." She stopped talking as she caught sight of the gray metal filing cabinets lining the side wall, remembering the red folder that had contained her life story.

"Where are you going?" Daniel asked as she leaped out of the chair.

"You print all this stuff out and then see what you can find on CCCR Deployment," she said, pointing to the last search term on their list. "I know what I'm doing."

But there was nothing in any of the filing cabinets about the Eve Trials. Nor could she find anything about herself, not under her name and not under Subject 13. J.D. slumped down on the floor, banging her head back against the metal cabinet. It didn't matter, she told herself. They already had enough to go to the authorities — *if* they could get out of the Institute. They could get caught at any moment; it would be smart to leave now.

But she just *knew* there was something more she needed to know. Some answer about herself, to a question she didn't know enough to ask. But if it wasn't in the computer and it wasn't in the files . . .

Then she realized she hadn't checked every file.

From where she was sitting, J.D. had a perfect view of a small black safe on the opposite wall, a few feet behind Dr. Sykes's desk. She stood up and hurried across the room, running her hand across its smooth metal surface. It was locked, of course, and the combination lock would be impossible for even Daniel to pick.

Good thing that, for her, locks didn't matter.

She rested her hand on the safe. It was hard to concentrate, knowing what might lie inside. But just as she'd been trained, she forced all her thoughts out of her mind. She closed her eyes, breathed deeply and rhythmically, and focused on the warm metal against her fingers, the thick, heavy door, the brittle lock holding it shut. She visualized the safe swinging wide open, then she dug deep. And *willed* it into reality. The energy surged through her, a warm, tingling heat crawling down her arms with a familiar pins-and-needles sensation. And the door popped open.

Ansel Sykes had trained her well.

"J.D., you've got to see this," Daniel called from the computer.

But J.D. shook her head. "In a minute." The safe was empty except for a single manila folder. A label across the top bore cramped, precise handwriting: *Eve Trials*.

"J.D., this is really —"

"*Wait,*" she insisted. But for a moment, she was tempted to listen to him, to slam the safe shut without reaching inside. That folder held the answer. Not the lies that other people wanted to feed her, but the truth. Only the truth would be locked up so tight. Only the truth would scare her this much, making her wonder whether, just maybe, she was better off not knowing. After all, her relentless search for answers had only led to more horror and more pain. But she reached into the safe and opened the file.

Even the most horrible truth was better than a lie.

terminated

The file contained a thick sheaf of papers, all filled with the same confusing strings of letters that J.D. had seen in the Galton Project files. But on top of the computer printouts lay a series of yellowed, handwritten lab notes, all dated thirteen years ago. Many were too illegible to read, and some of them were incomprehensible, even though she could make out every word.

But some of them were terrifyingly clear.

12/17 — GENETIC SEQUENCING TRIALS PROGRESSING. HAVE HARVESTED DONOR EGGS. MUTATIONS STILL A PROBLEM.

1/22 — MERSENNE DOUBTS ENGINEERED DNA WILL YIELD STRONGER TELEKINESIS; DISAGREE. HAVE MAPPED THE SEQUENCE PRECISELY, AND EXPECT MY ENHANCEMENTS TO WORK. KNOW THEY WILL.

2/12 — IMPLANTATION MORE DIFFICULT THAN EX-
PECTED. ALTERED GENE INTERFERING WITH PROCESS?

2/20 — SUCCESS! ELEVEN EGGS IMPLANTED.

3/5 — SEVEN PREGNANCIES. NOW WE WAIT.

12/29 — SUBJECTS 13A, B, C, F, G HEALTHY. CON-
CERNS ABOUT D AND E — MUTATION? BETTER THAN
EXPECTED YIELD. MUST REMAIN CAUTIOUS.

1/9 — SUBJECT 13E TERMINATED

J.D. swallowed hard. Maybe she was reading it wrong.

But she didn't think so. Seven pregnancies — and then, nine months later, seven "subjects." Seven babies.

Seven babies with DNA that Sykes and Mersenne had somehow altered. *Engineered.* In pursuit of what? A child who would be stronger, who would be *special*?

A child like me, J.D. thought, remembering how Dr. Sykes had treated her as his pet, his prize pupil. He'd complimented her on being so much stronger than the other girls, and he'd always seemed so proud, as if he were somehow responsible.

Maybe because he was.

The strings of letters were gene sequences, she realized, flipping through the file again.

GAA TGC TGC ACT TTG GCT TGC ACT TTG
GCT TTG GCT TGC GCT TTG GCT . . .

There were pages and pages of them, filled with scrawled notations, some crossed out, some circled, all of them, she realized, experiments that had failed — and, in a few rare cases, succeeded.

The successes: subjects 13A, B, C, D, E, F, and G.

At least until January ninth. When subject E had been "terminated."

It can't mean what I think it means, J.D. thought. *He wouldn't . . . he couldn't kill a baby.*

But even if the subject — the *baby* — had died naturally, because of whatever Sykes and Mersenne had done to its DNA, even that was unthinkable.

Even more unthinkable than the fact that J.D. had been designed. She had been *built.*

That's why they treat me like I'm their property, she thought.

I am.

She paged through the file, desperate for more information about what had happened to the other 13s, and it was all there, on a series of pages toward the back. Each subject had her own record sheet, which kept track of vital statistics over time — height, weight, blood pressure, neural output, and a series of other statistics that meant nothing to J.D. They were all dated, and she felt like she was watching the girls grow.

J.D. was more interested in the handwritten comments next to many of the entries, which increased as the girls got older.

SUBJECT 13A, "ELISE"
2/24, 2 YRS, 2 MTHS: SUBJECT SHOWS BETTER THAN AVERAGE MOTOR SKILLS, NO SIGN OF TELEKINETIC ABILITY
3/14, 2 YRS, 3 MTHS: SUBJECT MOVED RATTLE WITH HER MIND
4/7, 2 YRS, 4 MTHS: SUBJECT NOT SLEEPING, LONG CRYING JAGS
4/13, 2 YRS, 4 MTHS: FEVER FOR 3 DAYS, TEMPERATURE STILL RISING
4/15: SUBJECT TERMINATED

J.D. turned the page, but there was nothing more about subject 13A.

"Elise."

The next page chronicled the growth of subject 13B up until age three, when she began talking to people who weren't there. She'd been taken to the medical wing for tests on May 6. While there, she had, for no reason anyone could determine, lost the ability to move her arms and legs.

And then:

5/9: SUBJECT TERMINATED

J.D. couldn't catch her breath. And she couldn't stop turning the pages, much as she wanted to. Subject 13C had gone blind at age four. Subject 13F had a grand mal seizure when exposed to colored lights. Subject 13D had seemed healthy and strong until age five, when her body lost the ability to digest food and began devouring itself. No matter what the details, every record ended with the same brutish conclusion:

SUBJECT TERMINATED
SUBJECT TERMINATED
SUBJECT TERMINATED

Every record except the final one.
Subject 13G: "JORDAN," which continued for ten years. Jordan was, in every way, a healthy, normal, growing girl. Normal, except in the way that counted most.

There were no notes after age ten. Only a white sheet of paper with a chunk of text typed across the top.

Re: Eve Trials

Despite disappointments early on, Eve Trials have produced one subject, 13G, who consistently demonstrates a higher level of telekinetic ability than natural-born subjects. No sign of the mutations that contaminated subjects 13A through F; subject will be closely monitored, but should be considered a qualified success.

In response to query of 4/15 re: a second round of trials: Dr. Mersenne and I recommend against it. The new chemical stimulants administered to subjects 1 through 12 have shown excellent results, boosting their abilities to at least two thirds the capability of subject 13G. Higher levels than that currently lead to destabilization. But improvement should come soon. Recommend that attention and funding be refocused to encoding techniques. On current time line, subjects should be mission-ready within three years.

Ansel Sykes

"J.D.!" Daniel's hands were on her shoulders, shaking her. "Snap out of it!"

"What?"

"What do you mean, what?" he asked, pulling her up off the ground. "I called your name, like, five times. You have to see this. I found it in his desk."

She'd seen enough.

"Let's just get out of here," she urged him. "Before we get caught."

"Just look!" he insisted, and shoved a printout into her hands.

"What's this supposed to . . . oh." She should have been horrified, she thought, as she read through the elaborate descriptions of murder and destruction. She should at least have been surprised.

But after what she'd seen, she didn't have any room left in her mind for surprise and horror. And besides, there was something all too familiar about the plan laid out on the page. This was the CCCR Deployment file, the final term on the scrap of paper. CCCR, the Coalition for Civil and Cultural Reform, would be gathering in the city for an international convention of world leaders.

The convention would never take place.

The sheet of paper had a list of names — names of world leaders — and a list of "accidental" ways that each would die.

A list of missions.

One prime minister would "fall" out of a thirtieth-story window.

One ambassador would be run over by a bus.

One foreign minister would die when his long black town car ran off the road into a gas-station pump and exploded. *Subject 13,* read the notation next to the task. But she didn't need anyone to tell her what was supposed to happen. She'd seen it herself. She'd felt the heat; she'd smelled the fire. She'd seen the man's face as his world exploded around him.

One prince would be electrocuted by a downed power line. That task had first been assigned to subject 6, "ILANA." But it had been reassigned to someone else. "ILANA" had been crossed out, and next to the name, a small, familiar notation:

SUBJECT TERMINATED

A drop of water spattered on the page, and J.D. brushed her hand across her eyes. There was no time for tears. Not when there was so much more death on its way.

The final task, scheduled for the same day as the assassinations, lay at the bottom of the page.

> Subjects 3, 4, 8, 13: Destruction of Marshall-Frost Building. Subjects 3, 4, 8 stationed inside — maximum damage to structural integrity. Subject 13 — wall, ceiling collapse. Casualties estimate: 200.

There was a handwritten note in the margin, in the same handwriting she'd seen before, and she knew it belonged to Sykes.

> MAKE SURE 13 IS POSITIONED SAFELY AWAY FROM BUILDING (NO REPEATS OF FIELD TEST EXPLOSION!) — LOSS OF 3, 4, 8 UNFORTUNATE BUT UNAVOIDABLE. BUT 13 TOO VALUABLE, MUST BE PROTECTED.

The date of the mission was only four days away. Four days until she was supposed to kill a man named Goran Czernick. And then two hundred other people. Make that two hundred and three — because subjects three, four, and eight would be in the building when J.D. brought the roof down on their heads.

Ansel Sykes had built himself a powerful weapon, and its time had come.

"We have to get to the loading dock," Daniel whispered as they crept down the empty hallway. "There's a place we can hide until morning, and then we can —" They both froze at the sound of footsteps. They were too close — and there was nowhere to hide.

"Come on!" J.D. hissed, racing down the hall. If they could get around the corner and duck into one of the empty rooms, they could hide until it was safe.

"Stop right there!" a guard's voice yelled, but J.D. ran faster, skidding around the corner, out of sight — and only then did she realize that she was alone. Daniel hadn't made it.

Her heart thumping in her chest, she peeked around the corner, then yanked her head back. Daniel was standing in the middle of the hallway, facing one of the guards.

The guard had a gun.

"You're not supposed to be out at night," she heard the guard say.

"I was just, uh, looking for a bathroom," Daniel said, and J.D. knew he was doing his best to sound timid. He wasn't very good at it. "The one near my room isn't working, and I guess I just, uh, got lost."

"You got lost and ended up two wings away in a restricted area?" the guard asked skeptically. "You know this is trouble, right?"

"Look, I didn't see anything," Daniel said. "I swear. Just let me go back to my room, and in the morning, you can fire me, okay? Send me back to the Center."

"No one gets fired," the guard said firmly.

"I could quit," Daniel suggested. "Either way. Whatever."

The guard laughed. "Nobody *quits* this job, kid. You're not going back anywhere. You're not going anywhere, ever. Get it?"

There was a long pause.

Don't say anything that will get you into more trouble, J.D. silently pleaded, wishing Daniel could hear her thoughts. *Just keep your mouth shut.*

But that wasn't one of Daniel's strongest skills.

"What if I don't get it?" he asked, and the fake timidity was gone from his voice.

J.D. poked her head out again, just for a second. The guard was still aiming his gun.

"Why do you think Sykes would hire someone like you — any of you? Bunch of kids that no one cares about. Losers. No one notices where you go. And no one will miss you when you're gone. Which is going to be pretty soon if I —" The guard yelped as he flew backward off his feet and slammed into a wall. He slumped to the ground, unconscious, and J.D. stepped into sight.

"Come on!" she called as Daniel stood there frozen, with his mouth open and his eyes wide.

"Did you —" He pointed at the guard. "He was going to — and you — uh — how did you —"

"This is bad," J.D. hissed. "They're going to find him, and they're going to know. We've got to get out of here. *Now.*"

They ran down the hall as fast as they could, Daniel leading the way to the loading dock. But they weren't fast enough. Within minutes, alarms began to blare. The guards were on the prowl. And the hunt was on.

J.D. and Daniel ran down the corridors, ducking

out of sight whenever a guard passed by. J.D. didn't want to have to hurt anyone else, but she would do what she had to do. They were the enemy, she reminded herself. They'd kept the girls prisoners, helped train them to be killers. They weren't worth her worry, or her mercy.

But she still didn't want to hurt them. And she clung to that. Because she *wanted* to hate how it felt. Every time she cringed, every time she pulled back, it was one more piece of evidence that she didn't have to be what they'd made her.

That she didn't have to be a killer.

They made it to the kitchen, and Daniel pulled her toward the door that led out to the loading dock.

Dr. Mersenne stood in front of it.

They ducked out of sight just in time. "Did she see us?" J.D. mouthed as they crouched beneath a table together.

Daniel shrugged. They waited.

Dr. Mersenne wandered back and forth across the kitchen, as if she was looking for something. *She knows we're here,* J.D. thought. *She's just playing with us.* Dr. Mersenne stopped abruptly and stared across the room. J.D. could feel the weight of her gaze.

She can't see me, she told herself. *I'm too deep in the*

shadows. *There's no way she can see me.* But still, it felt like their eyes had met. Daniel turned to look at her, and J.D. could see the terror on his face. *He sees it, too,* she thought. *We're caught.*

She could knock out Dr. Mersenne, just as she had the guards. But Dr. Mersenne had her hand on a small gray device, and in a moment it would be too late —

"He's not here," Dr. Mersenne said into the device, then paused, as if she was listening to something. "No. I'm certain. The area's clear. We've swept the whole building, and he's nowhere. Perhaps your guard was mistaken, or —" She stopped again, listened, and then scowled. "It's of no importance. Call off the search."

And a moment after her command, the sirens stopped. She stared across the room again, and again, J.D. felt certain she'd been spotted. But Dr. Mersenne only sighed and slipped the device back into her pocket, then walked out of the room.

Daniel let out a huge sigh, and J.D. could feel his body sag with relief. "Let's go," he whispered. "Before she comes back."

But as they stood in the threshold — as J.D. felt the wind brush her face for the first time in too many days — she hesitated. Then she stuffed the printouts from Sykes's office into Daniel's hands.

"You go," she said. "I'm staying."

"What?"

"You have to go tell someone about what's happening here. And I . . ." She didn't want to be right about this, but she knew she was. "I have to stay here. I can't leave the others. In case you can't get anyone to believe you. Or in case something happens, and you can't — I just have to stay here. I have to stop this thing from happening, no matter what. I have to save them."

"I'm not leaving you," Daniel said. "No way. We do this together, or we don't —"

"This isn't like before," J.D. told him, trying to keep her voice from shaking. "You can't stick around just to protect me. You have to go and find help, but I have to stay, so we can protect *them*," she said, gesturing back into the building. "You know I'm right."

"You can't stay here," he said, shaking his head frantically. "It's too dangerous. After what we found out — and what if they know you know, what if —"

"They can't do anything to me now," J.D. said, sounding more confident than she felt. "Remember what you said? I'm strong. I can fight them. Especially now that I know what I'm fighting." She glanced over her shoulder, worried that even though the search had ended, someone else would come. She had to convince Daniel to go — and she had to do it soon. "You told me this was my fight," she reminded him. "You told me you trusted me to know what to do. So trust me now."

Daniel pinched the bridge of his nose for a moment and closed his eyes. "You sure this is what you want to do?"

"Are you crazy?" she asked, and even in the middle of her terror, a laugh burbled out of her. "But it's what I have to do."

"J.D. . . ." He grabbed her hand and squeezed it, then quickly let go. "Be careful. Promise."

"Promise," she said, blinking back tears. "Now go." She pointed toward one of the overflowing garbage bins. "You can hide in there until the truck shows up."

Daniel grinned weakly. "I always get the fun jobs."

Without warning, she threw her arms around him and squeezed tight. "Thanks for rescuing me," she whispered in his ear. And before he could say anything, she let go, slipped back inside, and slammed the door shut.

He'll get away, she told herself. *And he'll send back help*. But in the meantime, she would have to help herself.

She sank back against the door and dropped her head, letting the tears fall. She cried silently, her shoulders heaving, her lungs gasping for breath.

She gave herself five minutes — five minutes of misery, of terror, of desperate, helpless hopelessness. And then she took a deep breath and wiped her eyes. There would be time later to cry, and there were plenty of things to cry about. But not now. Now was the time to fight.

free

J.D. felt sicker with every step. Speed was crucial, she knew that. If she got caught, no excuse would fool Ansel Sykes. He knew her too well. She needed to make it back to the dormitory and back to the girls; she needed to get them out.

But she couldn't make herself go any faster. And she couldn't calm her churning stomach or relax her tightly clenched muscles.

I should have gone with him, she thought, knowing it wasn't true.

I could have gone with him, she couldn't help thinking. *I could have escaped. I could be safe.*

She felt like she couldn't spend even one more day trapped inside the white, windowless walls while Sykes and his colleagues experimented on her brain. None of the girls could. They had to get out.

Now.

She would tell them everything, and they would get out, *tonight*. Together, they would be unstoppable. Sykes had built himself an army, but he couldn't stop his troops from turning against him. They were too strong, and once they knew the truth, they would fight. And they would win.

She told them everything.

She described the brainwashing sessions. She explained how they'd been kidnapped and trained. She told them Ilana was never coming back. She repeated everything she'd discovered in Sykes's office, including the details of their upcoming mission.

Including the names of those girls who'd been chosen to die.

Sarit. Katherine. Brooke. Acceptable casualties who would do their job, then be terminated.

She got it all out, and then she waited.

The girls sat cross-legged in bed, staring at one another, none of them meeting J.D.'s eyes. There was a long, silent pause.

"I'm calling for help," Katherine finally said.

J.D. jumped to her feet. "Who do you think is going to help us? Didn't you hear anything I just said?" she yelped.

"We heard you," Sarit said quietly. "And, no offense, but you sound kind of . . ."

"Crazy," Katherine said. She came over to J.D. and pressed a hand to her forehead. "Do you feel okay? Do you have a headache, like, um, Ilana?"

J.D. pushed her away. "This is *not* like Ilana!" she insisted. "I'm fine. I'm telling you the truth."

"Then where's your evidence?" Mara asked.

"What do you mean?"

"You say you were in Dr. A.'s office," Mara said. "You say you saw all this stuff in his secret files. So where is it? Didn't you bring any back for proof?"

"No, I —" J.D. cut herself off. There was one part of the story she hadn't told them: Daniel. If they turned her in, at least Daniel would still be safe. Daniel would get away with the evidence and send someone back to help. She hoped. "I don't have any proof. You just have to believe me."

Katherine sighed and laid a hand on J.D.'s back. "Look, I'm sure it seems real to you —"

"It *is* real," J.D. snapped. "You're in big trouble,

we all are. They've been brainwashing you and lying to you for your whole lives!"

"Us," Sarit said.

"What?"

"Lying to *us*. You've been here, too, and you don't even remember it, right? You disappeared, you showed up with no memory, and now you're telling some crazy story about brainwashing, and you don't think maybe there's some kind of connection, that maybe . . ."

"Dr. Mersenne warned us that you might be fragile," Katherine added. "She told us to keep an eye on you, just in case, you know . . ."

"She's in on it, too!" J.D. protested. "They all are. They . . ." But she stopped. She could see it in their eyes, they weren't going to believe her. They thought she was losing it, just like Ilana had. And maybe that was easier for them to believe.

She forced herself to laugh. "Gotcha!" she said feebly.

The other girls exchanged confused looks. "Got what?" someone asked.

"Did you really believe I meant all that stuff?" J.D. asked, wondering if her expression looked like a smile or a grimace. "Like we're really super-secret trained assassins and Dr. A. is some kind of archvillain. Yeah. Right. Ha–ha–ha."

Katherine looked doubtful. "You don't have to lie to us, we only —"

"Come on, can't you take a joke?" J.D. shook her head. "It was just a stupid prank." She bit her lip, hoping it would work. They still took their medication every morning and every night, and J.D. knew exactly how it made them feel: content to go along, to believe what they were told. *So believe this,* she urged them silently. Because if not, if someone turned her in, Ansel Sykes would stop her before she could rescue anyone. Including herself.

"You're pathetic," Mara snapped, sneering at J.D. "Like you don't get enough attention already, you have to come up with some stupid prank?" She crawled back under her covers. "Leave it alone, Kath," she said. "If you tell on her you're giving her what she wants, more attention. Let's just go back to bed."

J.D. sighed in relief as the other girls began following Mara's example. They still looked like they weren't sure what to believe, but they climbed back into bed. "Not funny," Brooke said, shaking her head. "Really, J.D. After what happened with Ilana? Not funny."

"Sorry," J.D. murmured. She glanced at Mara, grateful for once that the girl was always so bitter and snide.

Mara was watching her.

And she didn't look confused or concerned. Her lips were curled into a half smile, and her eyes were narrowed. She looked thoughtful, like she was planning something — and that something was giving her great satisfaction.

She's going to turn me in, J.D. suddenly realized. *And not because she's worried — because she hates me.*

It meant J.D. had less time than ever to figure out a way to save them. *All of them,* she thought, tearing her gaze away from Mara. *Even if they don't want to be saved.*

She didn't think she would be able to fall asleep. But she closed her eyes in the darkness, and when she opened them again, it was morning.

It was early, and a guard was standing in the doorway. *He's here for me,* she thought in alarm. But before she could do anything about it, he smiled. "No class today," he said. "We've got a special treat for you girls."

And the music played.

As first, it was like before, and J.D. was carried away by the melody. But this time, she knew she could fight it, and that made her stronger. She let her body follow the orders — allowed herself to stand up and join the other girls in line. She marched with them down the hall, perfectly in step, swinging her arms in robotic rhythm.

But in her mind, she didn't scream. Not this time. She pushed away the fear and held tight to the thin cord of consciousness still linking her mind and her body. She pictured her hands squeezing a rope, her palms burning as the music tried to tug it out of her grip. And painfully, steadily, she forced her way down the rope, dragging her mind back into her body. The music played on, but she pushed it out of her way. *I am not its prisoner,* she reminded herself. *I am strong. I can fight.*

It began with her fingers. They trembled. And then, hesitantly, her right hand curled into a fist. *I did that,* she thought triumphantly. *I'm in control.*

She forced herself into her body, forced the music out of her mind. Her left hand made a fist. And then, without even having to work at it, she smiled.

Her legs buckled as she seized control, and she tripped, knocking into the girl in front of her.

"Keep going!" the guard ordered from the front of the line, without turning around.

Be careful, she warned herself, and relaxed her fists. No one could know that her body was her own again. She would have to play along perfectly while she figured out what to do next. And that meant following orders to the letter, pretending that she was still a zombie.

It was the only way.

The girls were led down an unfamiliar hallway and ushered through a doorway. J.D. almost froze as she saw the sun, but she stepped forward just before giving herself away. *Now I know how to get out.* They trooped across the grass, single file, emerging into a wide meadow surrounded on all sides by barbed wire. Trying not to draw attention to herself, J.D. sucked in the deepest breath she could. Fresh air — it tasted so good. Sweet and clean. It smelled alive. She shivered as a chill wind whipped across her face, but then she forced herself to stand still. The other girls weren't trembling in the cold or turning their faces toward the shining sun. They were standing frozen and staring straight ahead. Waiting for their next order.

Is that how I looked? J.D. thought, watching their blank expressions. She wondered if any of them were screaming inside their heads, struggling to break free, just like she had.

Or maybe the music carried them away into the darkness, leaving their bodies as empty shells. Maybe J.D. was the only one with the strength to stay awake and to know how it felt to be that kind of prisoner. After all, they were normal, and she was . . . something else. Something engineered, that even the engineers didn't completely understand.

The field was littered with elaborate metal structures, some dangling from small cranes, others piled on top of one another like building blocks. Ansel Sykes stood in the middle, smiling at his girls. "Number one!" he called, pressing something on his gray device. "Go!" He pointed at the structure to his left. It was a full-scale model elevator, dangling several feet off the ground. The elevator had no doors, and a mannequin was visible inside.

"Prime Minister Fuller is in the elevator," Sykes said. "Destroy him."

Mara stepped out of the line. She raised her arms, staring at the elevator. Four thick black cords

178

connected it to the low-hanging crane. They all snapped at once, and the elevator crashed to the ground. The mannequin was crushed.

"Very good," Sykes said. "Back in line."

It was a test, J.D. realized, as she watched the other girls play out the assassinations she had seen in the file. They were carrying out their programmed missions, one by one. And even though J.D. had read all the files and knew what was going to happen, she still couldn't believe it was so easy to make them kill.

Those aren't real people, she told herself. *They're only mannequins.*

It was true — for now. But if Sykes succeeded and sent his girls out into the world in three days, J.D. knew they would do what they'd been programmed to do. They would kill more than two hundred "targets." And then three of them would die, too.

She could stop it now. She could step out of line and turn on Ansel Sykes. She could knock him out, and then —

Then what? The girls were surrounded by guards, and if she made a move against Sykes, they would get her before she had a chance to make another. Besides, this was bigger than Sykes. The girls were programmed to follow orders, and anyone with one of those little gray boxes could guide them to their targets and order them to destroy.

She couldn't lash out, not yet. She just had to be patient. She had to be smart. But first, she suddenly realized, she had to figure out what to do when it was her turn.

"Number thirteen," Sykes said.

J.D. stepped forward as the girls before her had done. What now?

Dr. Sykes walked toward her, and she forced herself not to cringe away, even when he put his hand on her shoulder. "Ah, number thirteen," he said again. "Saving the best for last."

J.D. stared straight ahead, just like the other girls, but out of the corner of her eye, she could see the screen on his controlling device. It was lit up with thirteen small, flashing boxes, and Sykes touched his finger to one of them. The last one. A window popped up on the screen, and J.D. risked tilting her head down, just enough to read it.

Real Time
Mission 1
Mission 2

Sykes pressed his finger on Mission 2, and the music in her head shifted.

Then he pointed to a large concrete structure, about two stories high. It looked like a construction site. There were no walls, but heavy metal girders ran up each side, supporting a three-foot-thick roof. There were three mannequins inside, each positioned at a different corner. There were no mannequins standing in for the two hundred innocent people who would be inside.

"Numbers three, four, and eight have completed their tasks and weakened the foundation," Sykes said. "Your turn."

J.D. started to panic.

"Destroy," he said.

No. She couldn't. Not after working so hard to fight for control. She couldn't destroy on his command, even if it was just a model, even if no one would die.

This time.

She wouldn't.

But she had to.

"Destroy," he said again, and there was no more time to decide. She let the music take her over, let her body go, and it felt good.

A fire burned inside of her, a bristling ball of energy battling to get out. She let it.

The current sizzled through her body and exploded out of her. The concrete roof shook and she closed her eyes, seeing what had to happen in the darkness behind her lids, and there was a series of loud cracks as the concrete split, and then came the crash.

The building collapsed into a heap of rubble.

A job well done.

It was so powerful, she thought that night as she was getting ready for bed. The urge to obey, to give in, it was so hard to resist, even when she knew exactly what was at stake. How could she expect the other girls to fight, when they didn't even believe there was anything to fight for?

How could they escape when, with the press of a button, they would fall instantly under Sykes's control? Even if she convinced them of what was going on and they agreed to run, how far could they get before he turned them into an army of zombies?

J.D. sucked in a sharp breath.

She didn't know why it had taken her so long to think of it.

Maybe it was because she didn't *want* to think of it. She didn't want it to be an option, much less her only option.

With the press of a button, they would fall instantly under someone else's control. No argument, no doubts, no confusion. Just obedience. Immediate response to any order. All it took was a small gray device — and someone to use it.

I can't, she thought, repulsed by the idea. She couldn't *force* them to escape, even if it was for their own good. She couldn't become the person she hated most, someone who manipulated minds for his own purposes, who didn't care what he had to destroy to get what he wanted. She couldn't turn her friends into mindless, obedient zombies without the will to resist.

Or could she?

battle

J.D. started her search in secret, in the middle of the night. Before slipping out of the dormitory, she took one last look at the rows of beds, saying good-bye to the first real home she had ever known. If all went well, she would never have to see this place again.

It was the third time she had snuck into Sykes's office, but the first time she wasn't afraid of getting caught. She almost hoped for it. Staying hidden would be smarter, she knew that, but she was impatient. She was tired of pretending that everything was okay and that she didn't have a clue. Soon it would be time to step into the open and fight back, and J.D. couldn't help her impatience. She was tired of waiting.

She slipped into the office, crouched behind the desk, and slid open the top drawer, but there was nothing there but a few pens and a blank yellow notepad. The second drawer was cluttered with office supplies, and she dug through the rolls of tape and Post-it pads in frustration, but there was nothing else there. If she couldn't find a controlling device, she could at least retrieve more proof for the girls.

Get the files and get out, she thought, standing up to switch on the computer. But her hand froze in midair.

There was a figure standing in the open doorway, silhouetted by the light streaming in from the hall. "Looking for something?" Ansel Sykes asked in that familiar steely voice. He held up his arm, and J.D. could see he was clutching something small and rectangular. "Maybe this?"

He pressed a button and the room flared into light. J.D. flinched as the bright colors washed over her, shimmering and pulsing and lulling her into a zone of calm and tranquility, assuring her that everything was alright, everything would always be —

"No!" she shouted, tearing herself out of it. They were just colors; they were just lights. They meant nothing to her, she reminded herself. They had power over her only if she let them. "You can't hurt me anymore! You can't stop me."

"But this can," he sneered.

She heard the shot first. It was so loud she thought it was coming from inside her head, like the music. It was like the world had exploded.

And then she saw the gun.

I should . . . I should knock it out of his hand, she thought slowly.

Too slowly. Because she had already heard the shot.

And somehow, she was on the ground.

Time was no longer a flowing stream. It was a jumble of moments, sounds, confused images. All too fast, all in the wrong order, and she struggled to catch up.

The shot.

The gun.

The floor beneath her, and her arm throbbing, like she had landed on it when she fell.

When had she fallen?

There was a missing piece to the puzzle.

There was something red and sticky seeping through her right sleeve.

There was blood.

"You shot me?" she gasped.

There was pain.

Ansel Sykes stood over her, still holding the gun, a real gun, and it was still aimed at her, she could see into the barrel, the black metal shaft just wide enough for a bullet. And she knew she had to stop him, had to stop the gun, she had the power to do something, it should be so easy — but she was on the floor and he stood over her, and she did nothing. Because when she reached inside herself, there was only pain. There was no focus, no concentration, no pool of energy waiting to explode, there was only her arm, and the fire that burned across her skin.

"You need me," she whispered.

"Not anymore," Sykes said. There was no warmth in his voice, no trace of paternal pride. There was ice in his eyes. "You think I don't know when someone accesses my computer files? You think I don't know when someone is just *pretending* to be under my control? You think *you* can beat *me*? You're strong," he admitted. "But we'll make do without you."

Focus, she thought, staring at the gun, willing it away.

Tears dripped down her face. Pain radiated from her arm. Ansel Sykes smiled.

"You've caused me a lot of trouble," he said, "and I allowed it, because you are my creation. A testament to my genius, to everything I've accomplished."

"I'm not your creation." Her chest hurt with every breath, but she spit the words out. "I'm not under your control. I beat you."

He ignored her. "I've let my pride cloud my judgment for too long. There's no way I'm letting you destroy everything I've worked for." He raised the gun and took aim. "This ends *now*."

J.D. squeezed her eyes shut and waited for it to be over. There was a familiar feeling of drifting, the temptation to let go. Only this time, there was no music, only the fog, and the pain, and the fear.

She heard the sound of his laughter, low and guttural. J.D. tried to breathe, tried to move, but she could only lie there and shake.

Daniel got away, she had time to think. *Even if I die, Daniel can still save them.*

"You were my greatest triumph," Ansel Sykes said. "And now? My greatest disappointment."

The shot was like thunder.

J.D. screamed.

release

"Get up!" someone shouted. "Stop screaming, come on, get up, there's no time!"

I'm not dead, J.D. thought in wonder.

She opened her eyes. And screamed again. She was staring straight into Ansel Sykes's face. He lay on the floor beside her, his eyes closed, a purplish bruise spreading across his wrinkled forehead.

"Get *up*!" It was a girl's voice, and then someone's hands grabbed her waist and pulled her into a sitting position. J.D. shook her head, trying to clear her mind, trying to figure out what was happening.

"Mara?" she asked, blinking up at her rescuer.

"He shot you," Mara murmured, wrapping a piece of cloth tightly around J.D.'s arm where the first bullet had hit. "I can't believe he just shot you!" Pain stabbed through her every time Mara came near the wound, and J.D. jerked away, but Mara's grip was strong.

"Mara, what happened?"

"He really *shot* you. I heard the shot and I was too late and then he was going to shoot you again and I can't believe he —"

"Mara!"

"I knocked him out," she said, nearly hyperventilating. "I came up behind him, and I saw you, and I heard what he said, and I shouldn't have waited, and it was almost too late, but I, uh, I knocked the gun out of his hands. I sent it flying right into his head. It must have knocked him out. But I should have stopped him before he could — I had to hide, when I heard him coming, I could have warned you, but I didn't, I didn't think he would actually . . . I'm sorry, I'm so sorry. There's so much blood, but it's going to be okay, right? It's not so bad. It'll be okay. It has to be okay."

"What are you doing here?" J.D. asked, sucking in deep breaths, trying to focus. She pressed her lips together, trying not to scream, trying not to cry. She had to stay calm. They both had to stay calm, and think.

"I followed you," Mara admitted. "After last night,

what you said. I thought you were lying, just trying to get attention, you know? But . . ." She rubbed the back of her neck. "Today I didn't take my pills, just because . . . I don't know. And I felt kind of . . . different. When I heard you sneak out tonight, I just thought . . ." She leaned back against the wall, her face pale, looking sick. "It's all true, isn't it?" she asked in a hushed voice. "Everything you said, about . . . what he's doing to us? What we're supposed to do? It's really true."

"It's true," J.D. said, wincing as she climbed back to her feet. Her white pajamas were stained with red. Mara had said it wasn't that bad, but there was just so much blood. . . . She lifted her good arm and rubbed her eyes. There was no time for tears or panic. Not now that everything had gone so horribly wrong. "We've got to get everyone else and get out of here. Now that you know what's happening, we can convince them, and we can get out."

"How are we supposed to do that?" Mara asked, a little of her familiar sneer creeping into her voice. It almost made J.D. feel better — everything felt so surreal and out of control. At least Mara being obnoxious was a little piece of normalcy amid the chaos. Except that she was trembling all over, and there was nothing normal about that. "We'll never convince them, not in time, and even if we do, you said they can make us do whatever they want, that they just have to press a button and we follow orders, remember?" Her eyes were wide with panic. "There's no way to fight them. We're trapped here."

"Maybe not." Trying not to move her arm, J.D. walked slowly over to Ansel Sykes, who was still sprawled on the floor, unconscious. The gun lay a few feet away. She didn't want to touch it, but she couldn't leave it there for him to find when he woke up. So she picked it up, dangling it from her thumb and index finger. She'd never held a gun before. It was heavier than she had expected.

J.D. put it down on the desk and turned back to Sykes. On the other side of him lay the controller, a small gray box that could save them all. If she had the nerve to use it.

She picked it up.

"This is what he used," she said quietly. "To control us. And if I can figure out how it works, I could . . . we could . . ." She shivered. "We could get everyone out. Tonight."

Mara gaped at her, and J.D. waited for a snide retort.

"Do it," Mara said firmly. "It's the only way."

"You don't understand," J.D. protested. "Because you don't remember. It's horrible, it's torture. And what gives me the right to control them? To make decisions for them? I'm just . . ."

"You're the only one who can stop this," Mara said. "And you have to do it. Now. And J.D. . . ."

"What?"

"You have to do it to me, too."

"What?" J.D. shook her head. "No, no way. Now that you know what's going on, you know we need to run, and even if they come after us, you can fight, now that you know, you have to fight."

"I can't," Mara said quietly. "I don't want to. I just . . ." She looked away from J.D. "If you ever tell anyone I said this, I'll deny it, but . . . you *are* different. Just like they're always saying. You know how to fight. You like it. They're not like that. *I'm* not like that. And all this is just too . . . This is my home, J.D. This is my family. Dr. A. is — was — my family. And I know we have to run, I know we have to fight. But . . . I don't think I can. If you've got a way to make this all go away, to just let me close my eyes and wake up when it's over, you've just got to do it. Please."

J.D. looked down at the controller in her hand, then back at Mara, whose fists were jammed into her thighs. She didn't want to understand . . . but she did.

If someone offered me a shortcut, told me I could sleep through the hard parts, would I take it? she wondered. *No.* That was the easy answer. But was it true?

"Okay," she said finally. "Help me tie up *Dr. A.*, and then I'll figure out how this thing works and get us out of here. If you're sure."

"I'm sure," Mara said.

She no longer looked like the girl who'd called Ilana weak and pathetic, the one who'd constantly reminded J.D. that she wasn't as special as everyone said. She just looked terrified. She looked like she wanted to curl up in the corner and wait for everything to be over. Maybe Mara was right. She wasn't a fighter. None of them was.

Which means I have to fight for them, J.D. thought with determination. *And I have to win.*

chaos

They were an army.

An army of pale girls in white pajamas, their backs straight, their arms steady, their faces blank.

They were an army, and they marched.

Side by side, step by step, down the white halls. They were an army with power, invincible and undefeated.

And J.D. led the charge.

In one hand, she held a floor plan, stolen from Sykes's office, with an escape route clearly marked. In the other, she held a controller, *his* controller, the one that overrode all the rest.

It had been easy to figure out. Almost too easy. She pressed a few buttons and the numbers popped up on the screen, the numbers of her friends, numbers that were now the only identities that mattered.

She pressed a few buttons and turned off their minds — and when she spoke, she was in control.

After that, they were unstoppable.

Sirens blared. Lights flashed. The girls ignored them, because J.D. ordered them to. She ordered them to march and, when necessary, to fight. And the guards never had a chance. Every time a new one appeared, one of the girls sent him flying off his feet and knocked him out. At J.D.'s command. It was like playing a video game, attacking the enemy, guiding her players to victory.

Except the players were real.

The building couldn't hold them. The exit J.D. had chosen was sealed with four high-security twelve-inch steel dead bolts that sprang open only with a twelve-digit security code.

"Open it," J.D. said into her controller, and twelve girls focused on the steel door, exerting their will.

The door exploded off its hinges, and the girls streamed out of the building, into the night.

The perimeter security measures were all computer controlled, and J.D. had done her best to disable them from Sykes's computer. Hopefully, by the time anyone realized the problem, the girls would be gone.

I could destroy it all, J.D. thought, looking back at

the looming building. *We could.* They'd been trained to turn a building into a mass of rubble and to crush the people inside.

Innocent people.

They're not innocent, she reminded herself. *They all helped Sykes turn us into mindless killers.*

The girls stood motionless, mindless, waiting for her command.

J.D. wouldn't make them killers, too. And she wouldn't make herself one. She refused to let Sykes win, even if that meant letting him live.

"Follow me!" she shouted. And then she ran. Their footsteps pattered behind her. No one whined or complained or stumbled. She ran, and they followed.

The moon was nearly full, and it lit up the landscape with a soft white glow. The LysenCorp campus extended for more than a mile, across acres of empty fields and, at its eastern perimeter, a dense stretch of woods. That was the closest exit point, and the one that, according to the map, lay closest to a highway. The woods would give them cover for as long as they needed it, so that J.D. could decide what to do next.

I shouldn't be deciding for them, she thought, panting as she stumbled over the uneven ground. Behind her, the other girls' breathing was steady, their pace unbroken.

"That's it!" she shouted as she came in sight of the gate, even though there was no one to hear. The girls heard only orders. "We're —"

The towering barbed-wire gate was open, but there was a figure standing in the way. It was too dark to see the person's face, but J.D. could see her crutches.

They could find another exit point. They could tear down the gate anywhere along the way. Or they could stay and fight. One woman, on crutches, was no match for an army.

But J.D. did neither. She just stopped, staring.

"You can't leave," Dr. Mersenne said quietly. Her voice carried, and J.D. suddenly realized the sirens had gone silent.

"You can't stop me," J.D. said. "I don't want to hurt you —" That was a lie, she realized. More than anything, she wanted to hurt this woman. Wanted to hurt her the way she'd been hurt. *And I can do it,* she thought. *I'm the one with the power now.* She had all the power, and that was the only thing that made her pause.

Pause, not stop.

"I don't want to hurt you, but I will."

"No one's trying to stop you anymore," Dr. Mersenne said. "They think I'm out here taking care of it." She nodded toward a Jeep parked a few feet from the gate. "They think I cut you off, and I'm bringing you in."

"You're not bringing us anywhere!"

"You have to destroy it," Dr. Mersenne said, pointing back at the main building, which was just visible in the distance. "If you leave now, they'll only follow you. Wherever you go. They'll find you."

J.D. shook her head furiously. "I'm not destroying anything for you, not anymore. You don't get to tell us what to do."

"Think, J.D.!" Dr. Mersenne snapped. "You were designed to be sent out into the world — you were *built* to be controlled over long distances. *You* may have learned how to resist, but what about the rest of them? Walking away will never set these girls free. The music can find them anywhere. Unless you destroy Sykes's control entirely. You have to take out the main servers. And you have to do it *now*."

"You want me to believe you're trying to *help* me?" J.D. sneered. "After everything you've done? Please."

"You don't have to believe anything," Dr.

Mersenne said coolly. "If you're as smart as you think you are, you should be able to figure this one out for yourself. The servers have to be destroyed, or all of this is for nothing."

"I'm not killing anyone," J.D. said firmly. "That's your way. Not mine."

"The servers are housed in the south wing, in a separate complex — completely empty at this time of night. No one's in danger here . . . except for you."

J.D. didn't trust her, but what she said made sense. What was the point of escaping if Dr. Sykes could just press a button and call his subjects back to him the next morning?

She remembered being out in the world, hearing the music playing in her head. Wherever she'd gone, even when Sykes hadn't known where she was hiding, the music had followed. J.D. had learned to fight its effects, but she was the only one. So as long as it played, the other girls could never be free. And no one would be safe from their destruction.

Dr. Mersenne can't hurt me anymore, she reminded herself. *I'm in control. I don't have to do what she says.*

So when she turned back to the building they'd left behind, it was *her* decision.

It's empty, she told herself, narrowing in on the

two-story cube by the southern wing. The floor plan confirmed that it housed the computer servers, just as Dr. Mersenne had claimed. *That doesn't mean it's empty,* she thought. But it was the middle of the night. The staff should be asleep, safe in bed, far from the servers.

Except that I woke them up, she thought. Sirens. Alarms. Guards. There were people everywhere.

I'm not a killer, she told herself, again and again. *This is just what we have to do.* But there was no "we." The girls would do whatever she told them; they couldn't be blamed. It was her decision. It was her responsibility.

"Destroy it," she said, shivering when she heard the familiar phrase in her own voice. "Destroy."

They were an army, and now they had a target. They had their orders.

The girls lined up, and J.D. took her place beside them. She was one of them — she always had been. They stared at the server building, and she stared, and when she closed her eyes, she could see it behind her lids. She closed her eyes and she took one deep breath and then another, and she focused on what she wanted to happen, what she needed to happen.

She focused on the concrete and the brick and the

steel foundations. She pushed away all her anger and her fear and she concentrated on the building. And the building began to shake.

Twelve girls stared in silence, their arms outstretched, their eyes closed.

Steel buckled.

Concrete cracked.

Walls tumbled.

The roof caved.

The ground shuddered.

And where there had been a building, there was a pile of debris, and a cloud of dust.

Eleven girls began to scream.

"What's happening?"

"What did you do to us?"

"How did we get here?"

"Where are we?"

There were shouted questions and curses, but mostly, there were screams. Across a field, the sirens began to blare again, and a crowd of people streamed out of the LysenCorp buildings, and still, the girls screamed. They were confused, they were afraid, and they were on their own.

Destroying the servers had obliterated J.D.'s

control. Which meant Dr. Mersenne had told the truth — and maybe it was all true, maybe no one would be able to control them again.

"But why would you help us?" J.D. asked, turning around to find Dr. Mersenne and get some answers.

The woman was gone.

"J.D., what's *happening*?" Katherine said, grabbing her by the shoulders and shaking her. "What did you do to us?"

"We have to get out of here," J.D. said, still staring down at the chaos below, still wondering whether the server building had really been empty. "Into the woods. We have to hide. If they find us —" But what if? What could they do now?

"I'm not going anywhere until —"

"Listen to J.D.!" Mara shouted. "She'll explain everything, but if she says hide, we hide. Go!"

Maybe it was because they were so used to following orders, maybe it was because Mara sounded so sure, or maybe it was because Mara was one of them in a way that J.D. never would be — they listened to her. They followed J.D. as she retreated into the woods, crossing through the gate, then pausing on the other side.

She didn't know where to go next, or what to do.

And it was no longer her decision; at least, not hers alone. So they stopped in the woods, crouching behind a grove of low-hanging trees, and J.D. tried to explain.

"I had to get us out," she said, "and none of you would listen, so I —"

"You did something to us," one of the girls whispered in the dark. "Something . . . horrible. I remember."

"I remember, too," another said. There was accusation in her voice. "I couldn't talk. I couldn't move. I couldn't do anything but what you told me to do."

"I told you," J.D. said quickly. "That's what *they* were doing to you — to us — every day. I tried to tell you, and you wouldn't believe me, so . . ."

"So she got us out," Mara said. "We couldn't do it ourselves, so she did it for us."

"You're both crazy," Elise said. "I'm going back."

"Not until you look at this." Mara pulled a thick wad of folded papers out of her pocket and began passing them around to the other girls. They squinted, trying to make out the words in the dim light of the full moon.

"What's this?" Elise asked sourly.

"Proof."

There was silence for a long time as the girls peered down at the papers. J.D. wondered if they would be able to make out what was written — and even if they did, if they would understand. If they would believe.

But when the girls looked up again, she got her answer before any of them spoke. The terror was all over their faces.

"What are we supposed to do now?" someone whispered.

We escape, J.D. almost said. But then she realized, they had escaped. They were out. Her plan had worked. It was over.

Except they were still shivering in the woods, and they had nowhere to go.

Two of the girls began to cry.

"It's okay," Mara said, sounding like she was trying to be comforting but didn't quite know how. "J.D.'s in charge. She'll tell us what to do."

No! she wanted to cry. *I'm not in charge, not anymore! Stop looking at me like that!*

She didn't want to be anyone's leader; she didn't deserve it. Not after what she'd done and all the mistakes she'd made. Let someone else do it. She'd fought for long enough; let someone else take over.

There is no one else. They need me.

She pointed behind them. "There's a highway back there," she said, struggling to sound calm and strong. "So that's where we go. Someone will come."

"And then what?" Katherine asked. It was almost a whimper.

"And then we'll make them help us," J.D. said with certainty.

But what if that doesn't work? J.D. thought, a wave of doubt crashing over her. She shook it off. *Then we'll find a way to help ourselves.*

The fire trucks sped past them without slowing. But the police cars stopped.

The girls stood silent and still in the flashing red lights. Only J.D. stepped forward and handed over the stack of documents to the first officer out of his car.

The cops wanted to herd the girls into patrol cars and drive them away, but J.D. said no. And the girls listened.

Once the cops saw what the girls could do — one uprooted tree, one overturned car — the cops listened, too.

They couldn't just let themselves be carted away,

J.D. knew that. She'd spent too much time hiding, surrounded by secrets. And she knew how dangerous that could be. When your existence is a secret, no one knows if you disappear.

J.D. wanted everyone to know. The secrets had to be exposed; the truth had to come out. That was the only way to stop Sykes and LysenCorp from picking up where they'd left off. So she stood on the side of the highway as more sirens arrived, waiting for the FBI to arrive, as she'd requested. Waiting for the media to arrive, as she'd requested. And the girls stood by her side. As she'd requested.

This was power. She hadn't asked for it and she didn't want it.

But she was going to use it.

A fleet of black cars arrived, and the men in suits swarmed — but they kept a safe distance. There were cameras and flashbulbs and shouted questions, but the reporters stayed back as well. There was an invisible wall between the girls and the rest of the world, and no one was eager to breach it.

Until a silver car screeched to a stop on the shoulder of the highway. Two people climbed out, one of them carrying a large camera in one hand and a tape recorder in the other. Their path was blocked by police tape and a brigade of uniformed men, until J.D. finally spoke.

"Let them through," she said softly.

The man charged up to her, camera flashing all the way, and shoved a tape recorder in her face. "Eli Warden from the *National Investigator*," he spit out. "The world wants to hear your story, and I'm just the man to —"

J.D. stepped past him and faced the person he'd arrived with. The boy.

"You came back," she said.

"I promised I would." Daniel reached out to hug her, then froze. "You're bleeding!"

"I'm —?" J.D. looked down at herself and saw the red blotch staining her arm. She remembered the shot. It seemed like such a long time ago. And her arm barely hurt anymore. The sharp pain had faded to numbness. "Yeah. Don't worry about it. I'm fine."

"No, you're not, you're — J.D., what happened?"

She shook her head. "It doesn't matter. We're out. We're safe now."

"I would have come sooner, but I couldn't get anyone to believe me, just this guy" — he jerked his head at the tabloid reporter, who was recording everything — "but I should have tried harder, maybe —"

"It doesn't matter," she said again, and she took another step toward him, stumbling. He caught her good arm before she could fall. She was just so tired all of a sudden. "All that matters is that you're here. And we're here. It's over."

A man in a dark suit approached cautiously. "Miss, we need to get you girls somewhere safe. And you need to get some medical attention."

J.D. was suddenly so tired she could barely stand. She clutched Daniel's shoulder. There was a curious tingling in her other arm, the one that had been shot, and she suddenly realized she couldn't feel her fingers anymore. But she refused to show any weakness. Not until everything — and everyone — had been taken care of.

"You'll give us somewhere to sleep," she ordered the man. She'd gotten used to handing out orders. He nodded hesitantly, as if he weren't used to obeying. "But we *won't* be your prisoners."

"Prisoners?" He jerked back. "Of course not. You're just kids. You need help. Come with us, and we can help you."

But they weren't *just* anything. Not anymore. And

they would never be anyone's prisoners again. They were too strong, and now they were the ones in control.

J.D. twisted around to look at her friends, who were waiting for some sign of what to do next. "I think we should go with them," she said. "The government can't hide us away, not with all these cameras and all these people knowing we exist. Maybe we can't trust them, but they can't trap us anywhere we don't want to be. You know that. And . . . maybe they can help us find our way back to our real homes." *Or at least* your *real homes,* she thought. They all had parents out there somewhere, a life to return to. All of them except her. "But it's not my call. It's yours."

For a long moment, no one moved.

Then Mara took a step forward. "If you go, I go."

J.D. smiled. She wished she could reach out and take Mara's hand. But she knew if she let go of Daniel, she would fall.

"Me, too," Katherine said, joining Mara.

"Me, too."

"And me."

Soon they'd all agreed. And that was all it took. The cameras flashed and the men in suits escorted the girls, one by one, into waiting cars. J.D. stayed until they had all been driven off into the darkness.

"We've got to get you to a hospital," someone said.

"No." She clutched Daniel's shoulder. No more tests, no more hospitals, no more doctors. She was done with that nightmare.

"J.D., you've been *shot*," Daniel whispered. "Let them fix you."

"*No*," she protested, even though the numbness in her arm was creeping into the rest of her body. There was a little pain, but mostly just that strange pins-and-needles sensation crawling along her skin. And she was cold.

Very cold.

"I'm *fine*," she insisted. "Just take me wherever you took the rest of them."

"Only after we get a doctor to examine you," one of the men said.

"I have to go with the other girls," J.D. insisted. "They need me."

"Let them take care of you first," Daniel pleaded, staggering a bit under her weight. "That's the only way you're going to be able to take care of anyone else. Just let them help you. What are you afraid of?"

The question stopped her.

What was she afraid of?

Dr. Mersenne was still out there somewhere. Maybe Ansel Sykes, too, if he'd managed to scrape himself off his office floor before the authorities descended. She had no home, and now she knew there was no family waiting for her to appear. A horde of officials were begging to help her, but she knew better than to believe that people meant what they said, or were who they claimed to be. There was a bullet in her arm, and she could see the blood, but she couldn't feel a thing.

There was plenty to be afraid of.

And yet: She had escaped. She had led the girls to freedom. And with the servers destroyed, it was *true* freedom. She had brought down a building, just by willing it to happen. She had silenced the music forever.

There was an empty ambulance waiting on the side of the road. They wanted to carry her; she walked. Daniel stayed by her side.

What am I afraid of?

"Nothing."

hope

It wasn't a bad place.

The beds were soft. The rooms were warm. The food was . . . bland, but plentiful. There were locks on the doors, but that could only keep the world out. It couldn't keep J.D. in.

No, it wasn't a bad place. But it was still time for her to go.

"Mara left today," she told Daniel, feeling a twinge of sadness. "That's the last one."

They were sitting together in Daniel's room, two doors down from J.D.'s on the long gray hallway. It was a small room, with only a bed, a wooden chair, a dresser, and a small TV, but J.D. could tell Daniel loved it. He'd admitted that it was the first time he'd ever had a room of his own.

They had been in the government complex for three days, and sometimes, wandering its sterile corridors, J.D. imagined she was back at the Institute again. But this building was different. It had windows.

"Back to her parents?" Daniel asked.

J.D. nodded. The government had tracked down the girls' families and notified them that their children were still alive. Tearful, confused parents had flown in from all over the country, and one by one, the girls had all gone home.

All except J.D., who had no home.

Government agents had ransacked the LysenCorp headquarters, confiscating reams of incriminating paperwork. In every file, J.D. was known only as subject thirteen, the only successful result of the Eve Trials. There was no record of who her parents might have been. Ansel Sykes was in custody, but he wasn't talking.

"Think you'll miss them?" Daniel asked, leaning against the wall with his legs spread out on the bed. His sneakers had already left skids of dust across the white blanket.

J.D. shrugged. "I didn't really know them. I mean, I still don't remember anything that happened before a couple weeks ago, but . . . yeah. I guess I will. They were . . . like me, you know?"

Daniel gave her a sympathetic smile. "I know."

Except that they weren't like her, not really. Their abilities had been boosted by medication, and the government scientists seemed certain that once the girls stopped taking it, their powers would fade away. They would be normal girls again, just like everyone else. J.D., on the other hand, didn't need the drugs. She would always be different.

She would always be powerful.

Which meant she would always be valuable. And no matter how friendly the government agents were, no matter how much they talked about making her comfortable and finding her help, she couldn't trust them. Soon one of them would realize she wasn't just a child who needed their help; she was what Ansel Sykes had designed her to be. A weapon. And then one of them would decide to do something about it, to find a way to *use* her.

If they hadn't already.

"But it's good that they went," J.D. said. "It's good for them. And it'll be good for you."

"Are you crazy? I'm not going anywhere," Daniel protested. "Not without you, at least."

"Daniel, I know what they offered you," J.D. said.

"I made them tell me about the program. It sounds great."

He scowled. "What would I do on some ranch? Like I'm going to start lassoing cows or something? Please."

"No more Center, no more sleeping in abandoned apartments or empty factories," J.D. pointed out. "You'll get to be outside all the time, you'll get your own room, and you'll get paid. You could save up. So in a couple years, you could do anything." J.D. had insisted they show her pictures of the Sarafina Ranch, a sprawling complex of old-fashioned cabins nestled in the Montana wilderness. They'd shown her pictures of kids riding horses, kids climbing cliff faces, even kids herding cows. They'd all looked tan and healthy . . . and happy. "You have to go. You'll love it."

"Then so will you," Daniel said. "Come with me." He winked at her. "You know you can't live without me."

J.D. swallowed hard and ordered herself to keep smiling. "They'd never let me do that," she said. "They want me here to testify against Sykes. And then . . . they want to study me — they say I'm 'remarkable.'"

"Yeah, right," Daniel said, laughing. "I can pick a dead bolt in under sixty seconds. *That's* remarkable."

"Daniel, I'm serious."

"So am I. Forget them. You don't have to stay here if you don't want to. Just tell them no. Come with me."

"I can't," she said. Couldn't he see what would happen? "Even if I leave here, I can't go with you. They'd just track me down. They'll never leave me alone. Not knowing what I can do. Which means they'd never leave you alone."

"Fine." Daniel crossed his arms. "You stay, I stay. Together, remember?"

"No!" J.D. jumped out of her chair. She had to convince him *now*, because it had taken her three days to work up the nerve to have this conversation, and she knew she wouldn't be able to do it again. Of course she didn't want him to leave, but he had to. And she owed it to him to make him see that. "This is your chance, Daniel. Don't you get that? You can finally get out of here. You can have a *life*. You have to do it. I'll be fine."

"Without me?" he raised his eyebrows. "I've heard that one before. Didn't work out too well."

"This is different," she promised him. "The fight is over. We won. And okay, I couldn't have done it without you —"

"I didn't say *that*."

"I wouldn't have wanted to," she said firmly. "I owe you. Everything. So you have to let me pay you back. And this is the only way I can do it."

"By telling me to go away?"

She hung her head. "Yes."

J.D. knew she could have picked a fight with him, made him so mad that he would have been happy to walk away. Or she could have lied and told him that she, too, was going off with a new set of parents, and that she didn't need him to protect her anymore. But after all they'd been through together, she didn't want to lie to him. She just needed him to understand the truth. And the truth was that this was the only way. She refused to stay in some government facility for the rest of her life, letting a bunch of scientists run tests on her, trying to figure out what Ansel Sykes had created. Which either meant fighting them off, again and again, or slipping away in the middle of the night and living on the run. Trying to make herself invisible, while trying to survive. She'd thought of little else for days. And she couldn't come up with any other options for herself. But Daniel had another choice, a better choice.

"And what if I won't?" Daniel challenged.

"Then I'll leave anyway."

"Last time you tried that, I found you," he pointed out.

"This time, you won't."

They were both quiet. Daniel climbed off the bed and crossed the room, stopping with about a foot of distance between them. He was almost exactly her height.

"We'll keep in touch," she promised. "Email. Something. And I'll come visit."

Daniel sighed. "You better."

"You'll go?" J.D. asked, blinking hard to keep her eyes from watering. She tried to smile.

"I'll go. But if you ever need me —"

"I'll track you down," J.D. agreed. "I swear. And if you need me —"

Daniel snorted. "Help from a girl? Are you nuts?"

She punched him on the shoulder, but he grabbed her good arm and pulled her into a tight hug. Her wounded arm, which was in a sling, smashed against his chest. It hurt, but she didn't say anything. She just squeezed as tight as she could. "I'll miss you."

"Are you crying?" Daniel asked.

"No," she lied.

"Just don't get snot on my shirt."

"Then don't get any on *mine*," she retorted.

He didn't laugh, and neither did she.

"Thank you," he said suddenly, his voice muffled.

"For what? Turning your life into a giant disaster?" she joked. "Forcing you to go on the run? Almost getting you killed by evil scientists? Twice?"

"All of the above," he said. "And everything else."

"Just don't forget me out there."

"In case you've forgotten, you're the one with the memory issues," he pointed out. "Don't forget *me*."

"Never."

The hug seemed to last forever. J.D. closed her eyes, trying to memorize every detail of her best friend. She fixed his image in her mind: his playful half smile, the mischievous sparkle in his eyes, the way his brown hair would never lie flat. She promised herself that whatever else she'd forgotten, she wouldn't forget this. She promised herself that she would someday see him again.

And then she finally let go.

Daniel left the next morning.

The same morning that she found the letter.

It was in a white envelope next to her bed when

she woke up that morning, with no indication of where it had come from.

There was no name on the envelope, only a small, handwritten request.

Please read — before you disappear again.

She opened the envelope slowly.

You think you know everything. But you don't. There are more answers out there, and I can supply them.

You think you have no choices, but you do. And I can supply those, too.

There's a park across from City Hall. I'll be on the bench closest to the fountain at 3:30 p.m.

It's a public space — no risk.

I'll wait for one hour.

It was unsigned.

J.D. got to the park at four-thirty.

At first, she had decided not to go. Then she'd changed her mind.

She'd changed her mind again and again. But at the last minute, she hadn't been able to stay away.

Breaking out of the government facility had been just as easy as she'd expected. They couldn't hold her. Not once she'd decided to walk away.

The park was crowded in the middle of the afternoon, filled with children and families and balding old men feeding the pigeons. But the bench closest to the fountain was empty. The author of the note had promised to wait for one hour, but one hour had passed. Had she missed her chance?

J.D. sat down on the empty bench and stared into the fountain, which looked like it hadn't seen water in years. She was unsure whether to be relieved or disappointed. Missed her chance for what? She wasn't looking for another fight, and she didn't need to be saved.

"I didn't think you would come," said a cool voice behind her.

J.D. leaped off the bench and spun around to face Dr. Mersenne's cruel smile. She opened her mouth.

"No need to scream," Dr. Mersenne said. "We're in public. And we both know that there's nothing I can do to you anymore."

"I wasn't going to scream," J.D. said, taking a step back. "I was going to warn you to stay away from me." As always, just seeing the woman's pale blue eyes and sneering grin made her nauseous. "And then I was gong to call the cops and get you thrown in jail."

"What, no 'thank you'?"

"For what?" J.D. snarled.

"Are you forgetting who told you to destroy the server room?" Dr. Mersenne asked. "If it weren't for me, all you girls would be back in your dormitory, safe and sound, and under Ansel's thumb."

"If it weren't for you . . . ?" J.D. repeated incredulously, about to throw the woman's many crimes back in her face. There were wounds that wouldn't heal, she thought. Injuries that cut deeper than a bullet.

But it wasn't worth it. *Dr. Mersenne* wasn't worth it.

"I'm leaving," J.D. said. "*Don't* follow me."

"J.D., wait!"

J.D. didn't know why she turned around. Maybe because there was a strange, unfamiliar note in the woman's voice, cutting through the ice. Something like desperation.

Dr. Mersenne shook her head and spread her arms out at her sides. "You have to forgive me. I don't quite know how to start. How can I convince you that I'm on your side?"

J.D. spit out a laugh, then pressed her lips together in an angry line.

"Haven't you wondered why I helped you escape that night?" Dr. Mersenne asked.

J.D. refused to respond, especially since the answer was yes.

"And for that matter, haven't you wondered who slipped that note under your pillow with Ansel's password on it? Who ensured that your little friend Daniel got a job at the Institute, and who made sure he got out safely?"

"You're lying," J.D. snarled. "You would never help me."

"Who told you that you were strong, that you had the power to fight?" Dr. Mersenne asked.

J.D. flinched, and the doctor smiled.

"Yes, I thought you'd remember that. I wasn't talking to Ansel, J.D. I was talking to *you*. I was trying to give you the clues you needed to fight back. It was the only way."

"The only way to *what*?"

"To get you out of there," Dr. Mersenne said. "To set you free."

"And why would you want to do that?"

Dr. Mersenne smiled sadly and brushed a strand of

pale blond hair off her forehead. "I thought you might have guessed that by now. I suppose I thought there might be some . . . connection, something in you that might already know . . ." She shook her head. "Stupid of me. Unscientific. It doesn't work that way."

"What doesn't work that way?"

"The mother-daughter bond," Dr. Mersenne said quietly. "There'd be no reason to expect you to somehow know that you are my —"

"Don't say it," J.D. warned her. She couldn't handle any more lies about who she was or where she came from. Especially not from this woman, who had pretended to love her as part of a manipulative game.

"My daughter," Dr. Mersenne said. "And you are. Which makes me your mother."

"That's a lie," J.D. snapped. "And you already tried that one, remember? It didn't work then, and it's not working now."

"Why do you think Ansel picked me to play the role of your mother? It was more than coincidence. It was —"

"No!" J.D. shouted. She refused to believe it. Better to be an orphan; better to be Frankenstein's monster, a freak designed in a lab, than to discover her mother was the enemy.

"Look at me," the woman said. "Look at me and tell me you don't believe me."

J.D. didn't want to, but she couldn't stop herself from taking in the pale blue eyes, the color of an icy lake reflecting the sky. The silky thin blond hair, a white gold against skin so pale it was nearly translucent. The long, slim fingers, the narrow nose, the shallow dimple in her chin, it was all too familiar. She'd seen those eyes, that hair, the skin, the face, all of it, in the mirror, every day, watching her, waiting for her to figure out who she really was.

This can't be the answer, J.D. thought defiantly. *I won't let it be.*

"Thirteen years ago, Ansel Sykes asked for volunteers," Dr. Mersenne said. J.D. told herself not to listen. She told herself to walk away. But she stayed. "He was a scientific visionary, and I was young — and stupid. There were seven of us, all pregnant at the same time; none of us were told who the fathers were. And none of the children made it, except for you, J.D. You were the only one. You were special."

"That's why you *killed* all the other 'subjects'?" J.D. asked bitterly. "Why you 'terminated' the *babies*?"

Dr. Mersenne shuddered almost imperceptibly. But her expression didn't change, and she didn't look away. "I was in a much lower level position then," she said calmly. "I didn't know the full extent of the project. But as I began to see what was really going on — and as I began to know *you* — I realized I'd made a mistake. By then it was too late. The subconscious controls were implanted in you nearly from birth, you realize. Even if I'd gotten you out of the Institute, Sykes would have followed us. And you would never have been free."

"So you just gave up?" J.D. asked incredulously. "You decided to go along with the whole thing and experiment on your" — her throat closed up, choking down the word — "*daughter*, along with a bunch of other innocent children?"

"We were closely supervised at all times. There was little I could do. But I was always looking for a way out," Dr. Mersenne said. "It took a long time — nearly too long — but I found it. I came up with a way to counteract the effects of Lyseptican and clear your mind of all implanted controls, only . . ."

"Only what?"

"There was an unavoidable side effect. It would have been impossible to cleanse your brain of certain memories and triggers while leaving everything else intact, so —"

"You?" J.D. asked, rage boiling within her. "You're the reason I can't remember everything? You stole my memory?"

"We," Dr. Mersenne said. "You agreed to it. I told you the truth, about everything, and you agreed this was the only way. They were going to send you out for a field test, no close supervision, it was our chance. So I injected you, knowing it would be a few hours before the drug took effect, but . . . something went wrong. The explosion got out of control, you were knocked out, and I couldn't get to you in time. Ansel found you first. And . . . you know the rest."

"The rest is you worked with him to fool me into thinking I was going crazy. You lied about being my mother, just like you're lying now, all so you could get me back to your Institute and turn me into a killer."

"That's why *he* lied to you," Dr. Mersenne protested. "And he was watching me, the whole time, to make sure I played along. But I have to admit . . ." For the first time, she looked away. "I thought it might be easier for — well, for both of us. If we could make a fresh start. If you knew me only as your mother and not what . . . not what I actually am. When I put you in the back of that van —"

"When you knocked me out and locked me into a straitjacket," J.D. corrected her.

"I was going to drive us both away to safety, to somewhere he couldn't find us. But you ran away before I could tell you the truth, and the next time I saw you, it was too late. He'd already started to regain his control over you, and I couldn't administer the drug again. It would have been too dangerous. I could only wait and try to help you fight back for yourself. The process that destroyed your memory also made it impossible for Sykes to regain full control over your mind. You just needed some help realizing it. That was all I could do."

"Now I know you're lying," J.D. spit out. "Because if you'd really wanted to help me, if you were really my mother, you wouldn't have just sat around watching and waiting. You would have gotten me out. You wouldn't have treated me like a lab animal that should be put down."

"Ansel kept a close eye on me," Dr. Mersenne protested. "I had to play along. I tried to get you alone, but you" — she shook her head — "no. There are no excuses. You're right. I was a coward. From beginning to end. I did whatever I could for you, but in the end, you're right, I just watched, and hoped. Hoped that you would be stronger than I was." She took a step toward J.D. and reached out a hand, but J.D. jerked away. "And you are."

"Fix me," J.D. said suddenly.

"What?"

"If you're telling the truth, if you're really the one who destroyed my memory, then you must know how to fix it. Give me back my life."

Dr. Mersenne didn't say anything.

"Fix me!" J.D. screamed. The other people in the park were starting to stare.

"I can't," Dr. Mersenne said. "It's permanent. I'm sorry, but it's permanent. You knew that when you agreed to it, even if you don't remember now."

"I don't remember *anything* now!" J.D. shouted, furiously brushing away tears. She wouldn't let this woman make her cry. "And you did that to me. You took it all away. You ruined everything, and you're telling me it's permanent? You're telling me I'm going to be like this forever, just . . . blank? Empty? Nobody?"

Her legs went weak, and J.D. let herself sink to the ground. She slumped over in the grass, resting her elbows on her knees, and cradled her head in her hands. All this time, all she'd wanted were answers. There was a wall in her brain, impossibly tall and wide and featureless, blocking her from knowing her past, or herself. But she'd always assumed that somewhere along the wall, there was a door. She'd been sure that if she fought hard enough, she would find a way through. She would find her past.

And now, this woman was telling her it would never happen.

Whatever she'd lost was gone forever.

"You're not nobody," the woman said softly from behind her. "You're —"

"Yeah, I know," J.D. said bitterly. "Special. Unique. An invaluable weapon designed by an evil genius. Barely even a person. Just an experiment."

"You're not what he made you — what we made you," Dr. Mersenne said. "Not anymore. You're J.D. You've created an identity for yourself. You woke up with nothing, and you built a new life."

"Just go away," J.D. moaned. "Just leave me alone. After everything you've done, can't you just leave me alone?"

"No."

"Why not?"

Dr. Mersenne stepped in front of her and looked down. J.D. squeezed her eyes shut. With her eyes closed, it was easier to keep telling herself that this was all just another lie. That maybe there was still a chance that she could remember — and that she had a real mother, a good, sweet, loving mother somewhere out there, who wanted her back.

"Because I lo — because I'm your mother," Dr. Mersenne said haltingly. "And I want a better life for you. I have to make up for what I've done. I told you the truth once, and you believed me. You agreed to come with me. I have money, and I have a house somewhere far away, safe, where no one can find us. Where we can learn to trust each other. I can keep you safe, J.D. I can give you a home. You wanted that, once."

"You think I'm stupid? You think I'm just going to go with you? After everything?"

"They'll be looking for you," the woman said. "The government, LysenCorp, those men who tried to kidnap you. You're very valuable to a lot of people, and that's not going to end just because Sykes is in prison. It won't end if I'm in prison, either. I know you know that, or you wouldn't have come. You can live on the streets, hiding out for as long as you can. Or you can decide to let me earn your trust."

J.D. opened her eyes. Dr. Mersenne was still standing before her, reaching out a hand.

"I can't hurt you anymore," Dr. Mersenne said. "And I can't control you, even if I wanted to. I'm no threat to you."

There were lots of ways to hurt a person, J.D. thought. You could lie to them. You could make them believe in something, make them believe they were safe and loved, and could trust the world around them — and then you could rip it all away.

You could steal their past and leave them alone and unconscious in a heap of rubble.

Could it be true? she wondered. *Could I actually have trusted her? Agreed to let her wipe my memory?*

Maybe.

Maybe not.

There was no way to know, not anymore. The person who'd made that decision was gone — and apparently, she wasn't coming back. So maybe it didn't matter what she'd once thought or done.

I made a new life for myself, J.D. thought. *I'm a new person now.*

If the past was really gone, then all she had was the present — and the future. And now it was up to her to decide what she wanted the future to be.

"You don't have to trust me," Dr. Mersenne said, still holding out her hand, still waiting. "Not yet, at least. Just give me a chance. Let me prove that I can be your mother."

Trusting other people was dangerous. She'd learned that too many times. But sometimes — she thought of Daniel, and almost smiled — sometimes people didn't let you down. Sometimes trusting was the right thing to do, even when it was a risk. Even when it could mean losing everything.

She could survive on her own, she was sure of it. But was that the life she wanted?

"I don't trust you," she said, finally meeting the woman's eyes. They were glassy, like she was holding back tears. "I don't even like you."

"You don't know me," Dr. Mersenne said. "Not yet. But you can. If we start again."

J.D. didn't trust her. She couldn't. But she could trust herself. She was strong. She was powerful. And she was finally in control. She was no one's prisoner anymore, and she refused to be trapped by her own fear, afraid to do anything but run and hide. She had chosen an identity for herself, and now it was time to choose a future.

She could trust herself to make the right decision. Maybe she could trust herself to take a chance. So she drew in a deep breath. She wiped her eyes. And then she took her mother's hand.

Robin Wasserman remembers almost everything that ever happened to her. She remembers the names of all her teachers and where she sat in their classrooms. She remembers her first goldfish, her pink stuffed elephant, her nursery school nemesis, and the theme song of every TV show she's ever seen. Her friends find this odd. Her parents find it annoying, especially when she interrupts family dinners to say things like, "Remember fourth-grade Halloween when you made me cover up my pixie costume with an ugly brown coat?" But mostly, she remembers good things, which is why she's in no hurry to grow up.

Robin lives in New York City, where she writes books and sometimes rides her bike very fast through the park, pretending she's on a secret mission and being chased by the forces of evil.

As far as she knows, that's just her imagination.